To my mother

Chariot Books™ is an imprint of David C. Cook Publishing Co.
David C. Cook Publishing Co., Elgin, Illinois 60120
David C. Cook Publishing Co., Weston, Ontario
Nova Distribution Ltd., Eastbourne, England

STORM WIND
© 1994 by Cherith Baldry

Published by arrangement with Kingsway Publications, Lottbridge
Drove, Eastbourne, England.
British ISBN 0-85476-523-9

Designed by Foster Design
Cover illustration by David Moses

First Printing, 1994
Printed in the United States of America
98 97 96 95 94 5 4 3 2 1

Library of Congress Cataloging-in-Publication Data
Baldry, Cherith
Storm wind / Cherith Baldry.
p.   cm.
Summary: As rebel colonies wage a war for independence from Earth, Randal and his
cousin Veryan see their planet taken over by groups burning books and destroying
machines.
ISBN 0-7814-0095-3
[1. Science fiction. 2. Christian life—Fiction.] I. Title.
PZ7.B18175St   1994
[Fic]—dc20   94-30488
                                                                  CIP
                                                                   AC

CHERITH BALDRY

Kingsway

Chariot Books™
A Division of Cook Communications

The Six Worlds

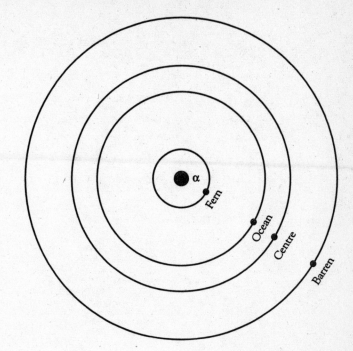

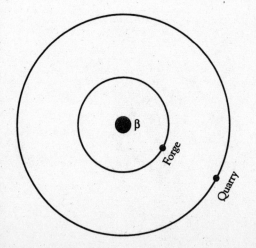

The Six Worlds and their two suns, Alpha and Beta, form a binary system. Beta takes several thousand years to make one circuit of Alpha.

This plan is not to scale.

Randal Gray picked up the boot, stared at it, and hurled it against the wall.

"I won't go!" he yelled. His mother's voice darted in from the next room.

"You'll do as you're told!"

"You can't make me!"

Silence was followed by the quick beat of his mother's footsteps. The door of his room slid back. His mother stood there, eyes kindling.

"If you think that, young man, then I suggest you think again," she snapped. Then she sighed, shoulders drooping, and thrust a hand through short, black hair. "Randal, please don't make this more difficult than it is already."

She looked very tired. Randal found it hard to go on shouting at her when she was face to face with him, but he was not prepared to give in. He sat down on the end of his bed and sulked.

"I don't see why I have to go to Altir and stay with my creepy cousin," he said. "Why can't I stay here?"

His mother took a breath. "Randal, your cousin Veryan is—"

She broke off. Crossing the room to his desk, she switched on his computer terminal and tapped the keyboard. A densely written page scrolled up onto the screen.

"Look—there."

Randal gave it a moody glance.

"Seen it."

He pretended not to notice his mother's face, the compressed lips, the straight lines between her brows that warned of a storm to come.

"All right, you've seen it. We both saw it when it came through. It's my orders, Randal. For the last three days, I've been part of the military. They called me up, drafted me. I haven't any choice. In another five days, I won't even be on the planet!"

"I still don't see why I can't stay here," Randal said.

"Stay here? By yourself? Randal, you can't even fix a hot drink without fusing the dispenser. And this room . . ." She stirred a discarded sweatshirt with her foot. "Randal, it looks as if a bomb dropped in here. You're supposed to be packing!"

"I don't want to pack. I don't want to go."

His mother let out a long, controlled sigh. "Randal. Look."

She tapped the keyboard again and a section of wall shimmered and cleared. The viewing screen showed the city: soaring towers patched with the green of parks and gardens, networked with the shining silver of the monorail lines. Only, across one corner, was an ugly gash of darkness where the buildings had crumbled and smoke still coiled sluggishly into the air.

"Randal, that was just one missile. It could just as easily have fallen here, in which case we wouldn't be having this argument. As it was, it took out the Barren control center, and incidentally, my lab. All the starship controls have had to be rerouted through Centre, and the scientific support staff have been ordered there as well. It isn't safe here anymore."

Randal had to admit to himself that she was right. All his life he had been used to war, but at a distance. It had been reports on newscasts and stories told by his father when he was on leave. Then a few days ago the first attack hit Barren. . . .

"Then why can't I come with you?" he asked.

"Randal, we've been through all this!"

His mother was hanging on to the last scraps of her ragged patience.

"I told you, I'm part of the military now. When I get to Centre, I'll be living in one room—maybe not even a room to myself. I'd like to have you with me, Randal. You know that. But it just isn't possible."

"But I want to be on Centre!" Randal protested. "I'll have to go there when I join the fleet."

"When you join the fleet! Is that all you ever think about?" his mother asked.

She got up and started pacing the room and came to a stop in front of the viewing screen. Her back was turned to the jagged arrowhead of destruction.

"There are other things in life," she said evenly, "than learning how to kill more people, more quickly and more efficiently."

"But that's what Dad does!" Randal exclaimed hotly, half getting up from his seat on the bed. "He's a fleet captain!" He hesitated. "Are you ashamed of him?"

The look that his mother gave him made him think that at last, perhaps, he had gone too far. He sank back onto the bed, muttering something.

"No, I'm not ashamed of him," his mother said. "He's a good captain and a brave man, and I'm proud of him. But when he was a fleet cadet, the job was trade and exploration, not fighting. Don't you think I would have liked to see more of him at home, especially when you were younger? How do you think I feel when his leave is over, and I wonder whether next time he won't come back? Your uncle . . ."

"Dad will always come back," Randal said confidently. "He's the best!"

His mother's lips tightened again in exasperation.

"Randal, I try to talk to you like an adult. So why do you insist on behaving like a child? Just finish your packing. You're booked on tomorrow's shuttle to Altir."

"But I don't want to go to Altir," Randal complained.

"And what do you think I want?" The explosion had come at last. "Do you think I want to be packed off to Centre like this? I'm a scientist, Randal, and I'm a good one. But for the last ten years—ever since you were old enough for me to go back to work—I've been developing rocket fuel. I have balanced weight ratios to power so that ships can fly farther and carry more weaponry. Do you really think that's what I want to be remembered for? Don't you think I could have done more with my life if we hadn't been fighting this stupid, pointless, destructive war?"

Randal ducked his head at the first blast and waited for it to blow itself out. His mother did not often get into one of these rages and they were soon over. Afterwards she was often sorry. And then, if he were careful, he might be able to get his own way.

This time when she finished speaking, Randal was silent. She rubbed a hand across her forehead.

"Well," she said quietly, after a moment. "There's no point in going over all that." She dimmed out the viewing screen and switched off the computer. "Finish your packing, Randal."

There was something about her very quietness that made Randal realize he was not going to talk her out of it.

"It'll be boring," he said. He was still sulking, but the words were an admission. He had given in.

"Would you rather be bored and alive, or excitingly dead?" his mother asked. Faintly, she smiled. "You're not being fair, are you? You've never met your cousin Veryan, but he's just about your age. You might get along with him very well."

"I can think of plenty of people my age who are—"

"Randal!"

Randal shrugged.

"Oh, all right. I'll go to boring Altir."

His mother really smiled at that and went out, ruffling his hair as she went past him. The door hissed shut behind her. Randal got up, retrieved the boot, and searched under the bed to find the other one.

In a muffled voice, he said, "Just don't expect me to like it."

2

Randal had been hoping that something might still happen to save him. Another attack. An earthquake. Or, least likely of all, his mother might change her mind. But the night passed uneventfully and early the next morning he found himself at the shuttle station.

The vast, domed building was crowded. Long lines of people snaked across the concourse. Men and women laden with luggage and small children were aimlessly pushing past each other. Yet there was not much noise. In fact, no more than a low mutter of voices that swelled from time to time and then died away, occasionally punctuated by the metallic announcements over the loudspeaker system.

"You're lucky to have that booking," Randal's mother said.

Randal understood. Since the attack, his home city—this quiet, orderly place where nothing ever happened—had become dangerous. People wanted to leave. For the first time Randal felt a faint twinge of fear. Nothing had been real before. Then he dismissed the feeling, impatient with himself.

"What about school?" he asked. "I'll not get into the fleet if I miss classes."

His mother, waiting beside the luggage check-in, brought her hand down hard on the table.

"Randal, don't start again!" she said. "I've never known you to complain about missing school before."

She turned away to answer a question about the flight number, and Randal took the chance to say, "But I have to—"

"For goodness' sake, Randal," his mother interrupted. "The new term doesn't start for weeks. If there's still an emergency, I'll arrange something. If worse comes to worst you can transfer to a school in Altir. Now please stop fussing about nothing!"

Randal was silent, seething inside. Even though he complained now and again, he enjoyed his school. He was going to miss his friends, and—if he were honest—the work. He did not want to go to another school. In Altir his cousin Veryan would be at home and he would be new and unsure of himself. Unnoticed by his mother, Randal set his teeth, grinning faintly. There might be ways of making sure that never happened.

Because his seat on the shuttle was booked, his luggage was processed quickly and he was directed into the departure area. He paused beside the gate, looking at his mother and suddenly not knowing what to say.

"You've got money?" she asked.

"Yes." Silly question. She had given him some before they left home.

"When that runs out," she went on, "I've arranged for you to use my credit code. Just don't go wild, that's all."

Randal was genuinely surprised. She trusted him, then, or perhaps the emergency really was serious. The betraying touch of fear returned for a moment. He tried to thank her, but she interrupted by hugging him, hard. That was something she had not done since he was much younger. Then she stood back with a tight smile.

"Take care," she said and started to walk off rapidly.

Randal called his goodbyes after her. He had not thought until then that he did not know when he would see her again.

When he had watched her walk out of sight, he went through the gate. One wall of the departure area was a sweeping transparent curve. When Randal looked out, he could see the shuttle waiting on the landing pad, its wings primly folded, blue and silver paint gleaming. No passengers were embarking yet.

Randal stood and looked down, thinking. He could still go back through the gate and follow his mother home. Then she would have to let him stay. No Altir, no cousin Veryan, no new school. Randal examined the idea; he liked it.

As he went on watching, he saw small figures begin to appear on the landing pad below. They climbed on board the shuttle. Startled, he realized that he should be with them. When missing the shuttle became a real risk, he knew that he would never dare carry out his plan. He raced for the elevators.

He skidded through the doors as they were closing, almost in step with a tall, dark-haired girl, who stood panting beside him. The elevator began to move downward.

"Hello," she said, grinning at him as she got her breath. "Were you stuck on the monorail too?"

"No, I—"

"It stopped between stations," the girl went on, not waiting for his answer. "I thought I'd miss the shuttle. They'd kill me if I missed it! Are you going to Altir?"

This time Randal managed to say that he was.

"So am I," the girl said. She stuck out a hand to him. "I'm Damaris Arden. You're not on the medical project, are you?"

"No. What project?" Randal asked.

Before Damaris could reply, the elevator came to a stop. They, with the last of the other passengers, had to wait while an official checked their identification. As he walked out to the landing pad, Randal found Damaris beside him again.

"Let's sit together," she suggested. "I don't know anybody else on this flight, do you?"

Randal shook his head. At first he had not felt like talking, but Damaris looked friendly. It was going to be a long flight. Her company would be better than sulking by himself.

"What's the medical project?" he asked again when they were settled in their seats.

"It's to expand the medical center in Altir," Damaris explained. "Since the war got close, they're expecting a lot of casualties. If Altir takes a direct hit like the one we just had here, they haven't really got the facilities to cope with it. And they might have to take in casualties from the smaller towns around. That's what we're going to set up."

"I thought Altir was supposed to be safe," Randal said. Damaris gave him a disapproving look.

"Nowhere's safe," she replied.

The way she said it embarrassed Randal, as if she thought he was a child or a coward wanting to run away. He kept quiet while the shuttle swiveled on the landing pad, taxied down the short runway, and flung itself into the sky. Randal had traveled by shuttle two or three times before, but he had never gotten used to the abrupt discovery of being airborne.

"I hate that," Damaris said.

The frank confession made Randal feel better.

"You're not going to do this project on your own?" he asked.

Damaris laughed. "No. All the real staff, the doctors, left a few days ago. I had to wait for school to finish. I want to study medicine, so it's good experience."

Randal listened as she went on talking, envying her because she had a real reason for going to Altir. He was just being packed off like a parcel. When Damaris finally got round to asking him about himself, he felt almost ashamed.

"I'm going to stay with my aunt and uncle," he explained. Because he was proud of his parents, if not of himself, he added, "My father's away with the fleet, and my mother has to go to Centre, to Derinath. She's a scientist."

Damaris took in this information wide-eyed.

"Your father's with the fleet? You must be worried sick."

Randal stared back at her. It had never occurred to him to worry about his father. But he remembered that his mother had started to say something similar the day before.

"He'll be all right, I suppose," he said.

He did not feel as sure as he had. Damaris looked as if she thought he was just putting up a brave front. She reached over and touched his hand.

"I'll say a prayer for him," she promised.

Randal felt even more embarrassed. He knew that his mother prayed regularly for his father. He himself said the right words when he remembered, but he had never felt that it meant very much. He did not know what to say to Damaris, but she did not press him. Clearly she thought he was simply reluctant to talk about his father.

Randal took advantage of her silence and looked out of the

window. They were cruising now. Randal could see the triangular shadow of the shuttle rippling across the padded surface of clouds below. He suddenly felt depressed. He wished he could be like this positive girl—sure of herself, sure of her faith and her place in the world. He wished he had something useful to do when he got to Altir.

Almost as if she had guessed his thoughts, Damaris broke in on them. "Randal, you wouldn't like to join the project, would you?"

He looked at her again, astonished. "Could I?"

"I don't know," she replied. "But you could ask—if you'd like to. If there is an attack they'll want every pair of hands they can find. That's for sure."

Her face was alive with the friendship she was offering him. Randal felt warmed by it. Slowly he felt himself beginning to return her smile.

"Yes," he said. "Yes, I'd like to try."

3

Randal stood in the shuttle station at Altir and looked around him. It was smaller than the one he had left. And at the moment it was quieter and more orderly. Through the windows he could see the gray of twilight. The glare of the artificial lights inside seemed very bright. His eyes stung. After the hours spent in the confined space of the shuttle, he felt stiff and stale. He longed to feel cold air on his face. He longed even more for a shower and something cool to drink.

Damaris had sped away as soon as she had collected her luggage. Randal envied how she seemed to know exactly what to do. Before she disappeared she had given him her radio code so that he could get in touch with her about the medical project. He would do that, he promised himself—just as soon as he settled in. Perhaps his cousin Veryan would want to join in as well. Perhaps the visit would not be such a disaster after all.

Randal would have felt more certain of that if he had not been left alone in the middle of the shuttle station. His mother had assured him that someone would meet him, but no one seemed to be looking for him. And Randal didn't expect he would recognize anyone. He stood with his luggage at his feet, thrust his hands deep into his pockets and waited, brooding.

After a while he became aware of a voice over the loud-speaker system. What had alerted him was his own name. He had missed the message, but a few seconds later it was repeated.

"Will Randal Gray please report to desk number ten? Will Randal Gray . . ."

Even distorted by the system the voice had an edge to it that told Randal this was not the first repetition. Wildly he glanced around him, identified desk number ten, and began hauling his luggage toward it. Beside the desk a tall man was standing. He looked frighteningly neat in a dark green uniform, making Randal feel even scruffier than he felt already. As Randal approached, he saluted.

"Randal Gray?" he inquired. "The Governor sent me to meet you, sir."

Randal muttered thanks. The man scooped up his luggage and began leading the way—not toward the exit doors and the monorail terminal, but to the landing pads reserved for private air traffic. Randal trailed after him. He had known, of course, that his mother's sister was married to the Governor of Altir, but he had never taken much interest in his relations or thought what that might mean. Now he could see that it meant very special treatment. Randal was not sure that he liked it.

He could not help feeling more enthusiastic when he saw the Governor's private flyer parked on the landing pad—a sleek little dart, filled with power. It was the same type that Randal's father had taught him to fly on his last leave, but a later model. Randal's hands itched to take the controls. He almost asked if he could, but the wooden expression on his escort's face as he held open the passenger door and saluted again killed the words on his tongue. He scrambled aboard in silence.

That was how the journey continued, except for the soft-voiced communication of the pilot through the radio. Randal consoled himself by thinking that his uncle would probably let him fly once he found out that he knew how. He peered at the city below, now no more than a cluster of glittering lights in the surrounding darkness.

Among the lights, almost in the middle, was a darker patch. As the patch grew in Randal's vision, he realized that was where they were headed. The flyer crossed a high wall and skimmed the tops of trees. Randal caught a glimpse of formal gardens before the flyer touched down neatly on its own pad. Beyond he could see the white walls of a large house.

The pilot opened the door for him and saluted again. Randal

found that he was growing very tired of being saluted every time he moved.

"The Governor's residence, sir. If you go in, the Governor is waiting for you. I'll see to your luggage," the pilot said.

Randal thanked him again, and set off along the path toward the house, trying not to show his misgivings. A set of double doors glided open at his approach, revealing a brightly lit entrance hall. Here a man was waiting. Randal had thought the pilot was tall, but this man was taller still, and gray—gray clothes, gray hair, flinty gray eyes. Randal did not need to be told that this was his uncle, the Governor. No one else could possibly have such an air of authority. Randal came to a respectful stop in front of him, not knowing quite what to say. The Governor spoke.

"You are Randal Gray? I have been waiting for you. Was your shuttle late?"

Randal swallowed. "No . . . I—I didn't hear the announcement. I'm sorry, sir," he added.

He had been wondering what to call the Governor, but now his problem was solved. It was impossible to think of calling him anything but "sir."

Randal followed as the Governor turned and stalked down the entrance hall to a room at the far end.

"We will eat at once," he said. "You must learn right away that I am a busy man, and I detest unpunctuality for any reason."

"Yes, sir," Randal said, subdued.

He struggled out of his jacket and handed it to a servant who had appeared out of nowhere. The man gave him a look that might have been a smile anywhere but under the Governor's chilly eye. He motioned him toward a door which proved to lead into a washroom. As Randal washed and ran his hands through tangled hair, wishing that his comb was not in his luggage, he thought twice about asking the Governor if he could pilot the flyer. He wouldn't ask. Not right away, at any rate.

When he was as neat as he could manage, he joined the Governor in the dining room. The servant was already setting plates on the table. Only two places were set. The Governor must have seen and understood Randal's start of dismay, for he said, "We shall be eating alone tonight, Randal. Your aunt is not here and your cousin Veryan has a tray in his room."

Was his cousin Veryan in disgrace, then? Randal wondered. It would not be very difficult to annoy the Governor enough to get yourself banished. Veryan might do it deliberately. Randal thought he might even be driven to try it himself.

The servant set down several dishes on the table for Randal and the Governor to help themselves, and then he left. The food was hot and the smells enticing. Randal discovered he was hungry. A little hesitantly at first, and then with more confidence, he served himself. He ate as he answered the Governor's queries about his journey, his mother's health, and the attack on the control center. After a while, he managed a few questions of his own.

"Will Aunt Anya be away long?" he asked.

The Governor looked displeased.

"I don't know," he replied. "She went to Derinath, on Centre, some time ago to teach a course at the university. Since the attacks started, the space shuttle flights from Centre have been canceled. I spoke to her by radio this morning, but there seems to be no possibility of her getting away."

He sounded annoyed, almost offended that his wife had dared to leave in the first place. Randal made no comment, but ate quietly while he considered this information. If his aunt were in Derinath he supposed she would meet his mother soon. They would both enjoy that for they did not often meet. On the other hand, it might make his own visit more difficult. Still, he thought, he might not be in the house very much if he were accepted on the medical project.

"I met a girl on the shuttle, sir. . . ." he began.

He repeated to the Governor what Damaris had told him about the medical project and her suggestion that he apply to join it. For the first time he relaxed a little, letting his enthusiasm break through. Not until he had finished did he realize that the Governor was listening to him with an expression of stony disapproval.

"You wish to join this project?" he inquired when Randal had finished.

"Yes, sir." More uncertainly, he added, "It would be useful, sir, and I'd not be in your way. It would be—"

"I'm sorry," the Governor interrupted. He did not sound in the least sorry. "It is not convenient. In fact, it's quite out of the question."

"Why?" Randal asked indignantly. The Governor's look of disapproval deepened to frozen annoyance.

"It should be enough for you that I do not wish it," he replied. "I hold a certain position in this city. It is not suitable for my family to be employed in servants' work."

"But it's not—"

"That is enough!"

The Governor was silent long enough to finish the food in front of him and push his plate away. Randal sat and seethed.

"However," the Governor went on, "there is another reason. You will not be available for this . . . project. You are not to stay in Altir."

Randal still said nothing. He was taken aback to be disposed of so coolly. If he and his mother ever went anywhere they discussed it beforehand. Even now when she had sent him to Altir, she had explained everything to him first. When the silence had dragged itself out uncomfortably and no more information was forthcoming, he asked, "Why not?"

The Governor sat, tight-lipped, watching him. Randal guessed that he was not used to having his pronouncements questioned.

"When I agreed to this visit," he said evenly, "I expected your aunt to be here. She is not. I am a busy man—more so in this present emergency. I have no time to be bothered with looking after children."

Randal sprang to his feet. His chair rocked dangerously behind him.

"I'm not a child!" he said hotly. "I don't need looking after! If I went to work with Damaris, you wouldn't even see me!"

The Governor's gaze raked over him.

"If you say you are not a child then don't behave like one." He got up and went to a serving table at the side of the room where he poured himself a cup of coffee. He did not offer one to Randal. "Sit down and finish your meal."

After a moment's hesitation, Randal obeyed. He pushed the last of the food around his plate with his fork, while his eyes remained fixed on the Governor.

"Where are you sending me?" he asked, stiffly.

The Governor rejoined him at the table and sipped his coffee.

"You will go with Veryan to my house in the mountains."

He seemed to think that no more explanation was necessary. Randal found that he was tugged in two directions. He might have been pleased if the Governor had not brushed aside his own arrangements so contemptuously.

"When do we leave?" he asked.

"Tomorrow."

Randal eyed him. He thought about renewing his questioning and decided against it. There were times with his mother when he knew that there was just no point in going on arguing.

"I'd better not unpack, then," he said, giving in. "But I should call Damaris and let her know I can't join her. May I use the radio, sir?"

Once again, without understanding why, he found that he was the target for his uncle's frigid stare.

"I see no reason," the Governor said. "The young woman was extremely presumptuous to think that my nephew would be able to take part in such work. I do not choose that you should associate with her any further. She should not expect it."

Randal was astounded. The idea of Damaris, frank and friendly and eager to do what she could to help, being dismissed with such cold hostility, left him at first without words to protest. By the time he pulled himself together, the Governor had touched a button beside him on the table, and the servant came back into the room.

"But you can't just—" Randal began furiously.

The Governor ignored him, brushing his words aside as he said to the servant, "Take my nephew to meet his cousin."

Randal stalked out of the room without saying another word. His mind was working at full speed. He had no intention of leaving Altir without telling Damaris what had happened. He would not let her think that he just did not care. Somehow he would manage to send a message.

He followed the servant down a corridor and out into a courtyard where flowers grew between the paving stones and a fountain played. At the far side was an arched passageway. Randal was just wondering whether he would ever find his way around when the servant opened another door. Randal stepped forward and heard the swish as it closed again behind him. The servant had not come in with him. Randal stood still and looked around.

He was in a sitting room, not the bedroom he had expected. The lights were dimmed, making the colors of the furnishings, which were muted blues and grays, look as if they were hung with mist. On the opposite wall was a real window, not a viewing screen. It looked out over the garden and the lights of the city beyond. The room seemed quite empty.

As Randal stepped forward uncertainly he heard faint sounds of movement from the direction of the window. A voice, sounding nervous, said, "R-Randal?"

In front of the window a large couch had been pulled round so that someone sitting on it could look out and would be invisible from the rest of the room. Randal walked forward and moved round the end of the couch so that he could see its occupant.

He found himself looking down at a boy curled up among the cushions. He was small and slender. If Randal had not been told that his cousin was his own age, he would have thought him much younger. He had a mass of dark copper hair, curling loosely around thin, pale features. His eyes, looking up at Randal with a scared expression, were deep and shadowed. He was wearing some kind of robe or dressing-gown of dark blue silk.

As Randal approached and stood staring at him, the boy put

aside a small book he had been holding and timidly held out a hand.

"Randal?" he repeated. "Hello. I—I'm your cousin Veryan."

Randal ignored the hand. He went on looking down in silence, more out of surprise than hostility. After a few seconds Veryan's diffident smile faded. He looked more pitifully frightened than ever.

"I—I was glad when they told me you were coming," he said. "I hope you'll enjoy staying here."

He had a slight hesitation in his speech. It wasn't pronounced enough to be called a stammer, just enough to make Randal think that the soft voice was going to fail on every word.

"We're not staying here, are we?" he responded resentfully. "The Governor said we're leaving for the mountains tomorrow."

"Oh, yes. You'll like it there," Veryan promised. "Everyone does. It's very beautiful."

He had withdrawn the hand he had held out and now sat twisting his fingers together nervously.

"Do you want to sit down?" he asked.

"No." Randal moved across to the window, but in the darkness there was not much to see. He wondered what Veryan had been looking at. "Have you a radio extension?" he asked abruptly. "Can I—"

He broke off. Outside, a dazzling, sulphurous flare arrowed across the sky, and vanished behind the distant line of rooftops. A second flare followed it. Randal blinked on bright gashes behind his eyes. He thought he could make out the distant thunderclap of impact. Behind him he heard a frightened cry from Veryan.

"What's happening? Randal, what is it?"

Randal pressed himself against the window, staring out.

"They're attacking!" he breathed out. "They're attacking Altir!"

Randal heard a stifled sob from Veryan. He cast a glance back at him and saw him shrinking back among his cushions, one hand pressed to his mouth, his eyes wide with terror.

"What shall we do?" he asked.

"Nothing," Randal said.

Looking out again, he could see a subdued shimmer in the air around the house which told him that someone had switched on defense screening. His opinion of the Governor's importance went up a notch. Not many private houses were screened; it would take a direct, drawn-out attack to get through it.

Beyond the sparkle, the sky had begun to glow dull red. Fire was somewhere in the city, but distant as yet. Nothing had followed the first two flares; Randal began to think the attack was over, or that Altir had caught the edge of a barrage meant for somewhere else.

Then the darkness was sliced by a thin, silver beam, angled like a searchlight, probing down into the depths of the city.

"What's that?" Veryan whispered.

"Rapier beam."

Randal had never seen one before, but his father had told him enough about them. Powerful, precise: they could be aimed from a ship in orbit so accurately that they could target a single building. Randal felt a tightness in his throat. He was not at all sure that the house shielding would stand up to that.

From the direction of the beam came a sound like ripping cloth, faint only because of the distance. Flames leapt briefly into the sky, leaving behind a patch of incandescence on the horizon.

"What's over there?" Randal asked, guessing that whatever it had been, it was not there any longer.

"The spaceport."

Randal understood. The attack on his home had targeted the spaceport and the planetary control center. Destroy ground support for the fleet, and soon the fleet itself would be ineffective. He wondered where his father was and what he was doing.

He stayed by the window for some minutes longer, but nothing else happened except that the shimmer of the defense screen faded. The attack must be over. Relaxing, Randal turned back to Veryan. His cousin was shivering, his breath coming in shallow, uneven gasps. He looked so white Randal thought he might faint.

"It's all right," he said contemptuously. "It's all over."

Veryan looked up at him doubtfully and then turned his head away. He said nothing—ashamed of himself, Randal guessed, for making such a fuss about nothing.

Determined to show that it would take more than a distant attack to bother him, Randal said, "I was asking you about the radio. Can I use it?"

Confused at first, Veryan barely seemed to understand what he was saying. Randal had started to repeat it when Veryan gasped out, "Yes—yes, of course."

He got up and crossed the room. A panel slid back at the touch of a switch to show the radio screen and keyboard.

"Do you want to call your mother?" Veryan asked. He was making some kind of effort now to control himself, but he still looked shaken. "Do you know the code?"

The idea of calling his mother had never crossed Randal's mind, but he thought he had better do it. She was sure to hear about the attack on Altir. However, when he fed in his home code the screen remained blank. When he heard the recording machine cut in, he left a message saying that he was safe. Then, as Veryan had withdrawn to his couch again, Randal fed in Damaris's code without offering any more explanations.

At first there was some interference, a frizzling sound and irregular flashes on the screen. Then it cleared to show him

Damaris's face. She was looking agitated.

"Randal! Is this urgent? We're at sixes and sevens here, and . . . "
Randal interrupted.

"Damaris, I'm sorry. I had to call you. I'm not going to be able to make it."

Her agitated look changed to annoyance.

"Is that all? Randal, we just had an attack here, or haven't you noticed? If you . . . "

"I'd be there to help if I could," he explained, interrupting again. "But I'm leaving Altir tomorrow. I have to go with my cousin. . . ."

As he spoke, Damaris tried to smile at him, but he knew her real attention was somewhere else.

"I'm sorry, Randal," she said. "It would have been fun. Listen, when you come back, give me a call. But sign off now, we really need this line."

"Yes, I—"

The screen abruptly dimmed out. Randal stared at it for a minute, frustrated. Then he touched the switch to let the panel slide back. Reluctantly he moved back toward Veryan.

Veryan was curled up on the couch again. He shot a brief glance at Randal as he came closer. He was faintly flushed. Veryan could not have helped overhearing the call. He knew there was something Randal would rather have been doing and someone else whose company he would have preferred. Even worse, he must have heard Randal dismissed as if he were no more than a nuisance. Randal felt his anger gathering again.

"I—I'm sorry," Veryan said miserably. When Randal did not respond, he ventured, "I didn't know you had any friends in Altir."

"You don't know anything. And why should you?" Randal's voice was savage, and Veryan flinched as if he'd been slapped in the face. "Leave me alone, can't you?"

"I'm sorry!" Veryan repeated. He sounded as if he were going to burst into tears. Randal turned his back and stared unseeingly out of the window. Behind him he heard the soft swish of the door opening and saw the rectangle of brighter light reflected in the glass. The Governor strode into the room.

"I've been called out to the . . ." He began speaking and broke off as he caught sight of the tearful Veryan. "Good heavens, boy, what's the matter with you?" he asked. "Pull yourself together. The house is screened. You know that. You're not in any danger."

His voice was scathing, his eyes hard. Veryan's face flushed red as he brushed a hand across his eyes, murmuring something inaudible.

"If you make yourself ill," the Governor went on, "you won't be fit to fly tomorrow and I shall have to reschedule all my arrangements." His glance turned to Randal. "I hope you've changed your mind about wanting to stay in Altir."

Randal clamped his mouth shut on the retort he would have liked to make. He was not going to give the Governor the satisfaction of arguing with him, even if what he wanted more than anything was the chance to stay in Altir and show Damaris that he could be useful.

The Governor did not wait for a reply.

"I came to say that I've been called over to the spaceport," he said. "There's serious damage there. I don't know when I'll be back. Get to bed," he ordered. "And don't forget your medication."

He strode out again and the door hissed shut behind him. He left a tingling silence. Eventually, Randal broke it, feeling uncomfortable.

"What did he mean, 'make yourself ill'?"

Veryan had sunk back among his cushions, limp and defeated. He shrugged.

"I'm always ill," he said drearily. "No one can do anything. You don't have to feel sorry for me."

The last words were a tiny breath of defiance. Coupled with the Governor's open contempt, they made Randal feel a little warmer toward Veryan.

Awkwardly, he said, "You might feel better in the mountains. We can go climbing together. Is there anywhere to swim? Because—"

Veryan was shaking his head.

"I can't do those things. They say I'm not strong enough."

"What will you do, then?" Randal asked, surprised into sympathy.

"Oh, the Governor has engaged a tutor."

For a second Randal wondered why Veryan said 'the Governor,' and not 'my father,' but he was too concerned about the rest of what he had said to pay much attention.

"A what?" he asked dangerously. Veryan had not picked up his tone.

"A tutor," he repeated. "You didn't think he would let us go by ourselves, did you? I can't go to school, so I always have a tutor. This one is new. They never stay very long. I suppose . . ."

His voice died away as he caught Randal's growing fury.

"Do you mean," Randal asked, the first stirrings of friendship swept away in outrage, "that I'm being sent up into the mountains to work?"

I don't need a tutor," Randal said. "I got good grades in school. The summer holidays aren't for working."

He had been saying the same thing to anyone who would listen since the previous evening when Veryan had first told him about the tutor. No one had paid much attention. Now he was standing with Veryan in the entrance hall of the Governor's house, waiting for their luggage to be loaded into the flyer.

Veryan glanced at him nervously.

"I'm sorry, Randal," he said. "I don't really have terms and summer holidays, you see." He sighed faintly. "I wish I did. It must be easier to learn with a lot of other people all doing the same thing. I know I'm dreadfully weak in computer studies."

And everything else, Randal thought, but did not say aloud. His own grievance still uppermost in his mind, he was beginning to speak again when one of the doors that opened to the hall slid back and the Governor appeared. He had another man with him—a stranger to Randal—and was speaking to him over his shoulder as he stepped into the hall.

". . . remember that my son's health is poor. You will no doubt find his abilities limited, but you will know best what to do about that."

Even though he had been thinking much the same about Veryan, Randal felt an uncomfortable little jolt to think that the Governor would say something so coldly contemptuous in his son's hearing. He shot a glance at Veryan and saw that his cousin had flushed faintly. He was standing with eyes cast down, pretending he had not heard.

The man with the Governor inclined his head slightly and

said nothing. His face gave nothing away. Randal eyed him curiously. He was a compact, dark man, younger than Randal had expected. The most conspicuous thing about him was a scar on the right side of his face, drawing his mouth up into a sneer. As he moved into the hall after the Governor, Randal saw that he walked with a limp on that side.

"Veryan, Randal," the Governor said, "this is your tutor, Commander Farre."

Randal's resentment fell away. Commander was a fleet rank. But how had the Governor managed to persuade a fleet officer into becoming his son's tutor? Suddenly enthusiastic, he stepped forward and held out a hand.

"Are you in the fleet, sir?" he asked. "My father is. . . ."

"I was."

The tone was unfriendly. Too late, Randal realized. The scar, the limp—the Commander must have been injured in action and discharged as unfit.

"I'm sorry, sir," Randal said. "I'd like to—"

"This is my nephew Randal," the Governor interrupted. "He has yet to learn when to speak and when to be silent. And this is my son Veryan." Veryan murmured something inaudible.

The Governor went on, "I believe the flyer will be ready. You had better leave at once." He led the way out of the house and along the path to the landing pad. The green-uniformed pilot was there checking the instruments, but as soon as he saw the Governor he slid to the ground and gave his place to the Commander.

"Get in," the Governor snapped at Randal.

Randal obeyed, followed by Veryan. If there was any friendly farewell between Veryan and his father, Randal did not see it. He fastened his seat belt and watched Veryan nervously fumbling with his.

"It's not a long flight," Veryan informed him, and added timidly, "do you enjoy flying?"

"Not so much on the shuttle," Randal replied. "But I like these." He could not resist adding, "My father taught me to fly one the last time he was on leave." Veryan looked at him admiringly.

"That must have been wonderful. Oh, I wish I . . ."

He broke off with a tiny, embarrassed shrug, and turned away to look out of the window. The Governor had finished his last-minute instructions and stepped back. The Commander cut in the flyer's engine. Smoothly, obediently, the tiny craft rose, hung poised for a moment above the garden, and then flashed out over the city.

Randal stared out, looking for damage from the previous night's attack. Then he realized they were moving in the wrong direction. Soon they were skimming over the rooftops on the outskirts of Altir. The country beyond was grassland, gently swelling, rising to wooded hills. It was pleasant, but not very interesting. Randal sat back in his seat.

Beside him, Veryan had touched the control to make his seat recline and was lying back, already looking half asleep. In his hands he was clasping loosely the small book he had been reading when Randal came to his room the night before. Randal peered at it surreptitiously. It was a Bible. Disgusted, he looked away, experiencing some of the embarrassment he had felt when Damaris had promised to pray for his father. Reading the Bible was all very well, but not from choice, and not when something far more interesting was going on.

Now that the flyer had reached its cruising height, Randal scrambled forward into the co-pilot's seat beside Commander Farre.

"May I take the controls, sir?"

The Commander gave him a sharp glance. "No."

"But sir, my father taught me how," Randal protested. "I have a novice license."

"And I'm responsible for your safety—for both of you." The Commander's voice was crisp, not to be argued with. But then his expression softened a little. "Not now, Randal, but when we get where we're going, I'll take you up for a practice flight."

It was not what Randal wanted, but he knew it was all he was going to get. And he was honest enough to admit to himself that the Commander had a point. Timid little Veryan would probably be scared out of his wits at the very thought of someone else at the controls. Randal decided to make the best of things.

"Thank you, sir," he said. After a pause, in which the Commander concentrated on his flying, Randal added, "My father is captain of the *Pioneer*, sir. Captain Gray. Do you know him?"

"We've never met." The Commander was still discouragingly curt. "But I know of him."

"I'm going to be a cadet next year," Randal went on, refusing to be discouraged. "Well, if they accept me. One day, I'll be a captain, too!"

"I'm sure I hope you will."

There was a sarcastic edge to the Commander's voice, almost as if he meant the exact opposite of what he said. Randal studied him unobtrusively. The Commander's undamaged profile was turned to him, so it was hard for Randal to picture the disfiguring scar. He wondered what had happened for the Commander to be injured like that.

"What was your ship, sir?" he asked.

The Commander's mouth tightened. Randal wondered if he were going to answer. Then he said, "The *Valiant*. I was First Officer."

"Were you in a battle, sir?"

For a second the Commander swiveled toward him so that Randal caught sight of the ruined side of his face—the eternal sneer—before he gave his attention to their flight again.

In a voice so level, so quiet, that Randal would not have believed it could hold such a cutting edge, he said, "The *Valiant* was blown apart. My best friend got me into an escape pod. We were picked up after two days, but by then he was dead. Excuse me if I don't go into detail."

Randal was silent. He found it hard to think of anything to say, but at last he ventured, "I—I'm sorry, sir. But at least you know you did what you had to. You can be proud of . . ."

He broke off as he saw once more that betraying tightening of the Commander's mouth. Somehow he had said the wrong thing. He wished he had never started this conversation in the first place.

The Commander's voice when he spoke was brisk and businesslike.

"Randal."

"Sir?"

"Tell me, Randal, why are we fighting this war?"

Randal was mystified—not by the question. Everyone knew the answer to that. But he was wondering why Commander Farre should ask it.

"We're on the side of Earth, sir."

"What's Earth?"

Now Randal did stare at him. Everybody knew that, too.

"It's our home world, sir. We all come from Earth."

"Do we? Where were you born, Randal?"

"Here, sir, on Barren."

The Commander's mouth moved into a savage smile. "I'm from Centre myself. So was my father. My grandmother was born on Ocean and she moved to Centre when she married my grandfather. How many generations do you have to go back before you come to one of your ancestors who was born on Earth and not one of the Six Worlds?"

"Yes, sir, but . . ."

"We're an Earth colony, Randal, but only a tiny handful of people from the Six Worlds have ever traveled to Earth. We don't import anything from Earth—nothing worth mentioning. Not produce, or people, or ideas. So now why are we fighting this war, Randal? Who is the enemy?"

Randal took a deep breath. He was not stupid. He could see what the Commander was getting at by now and he was not at all sure that he liked it.

"Rebel colonies, sir. People who don't want to be ruled by Earth anymore."

The Commander gave a swift, approving nod. "Good. So why are we fighting for Earth? What would it take, do you think, for the Six Worlds to be on the other side? Then we would still be fighting a war, but Earth would be the enemy. At the end of it we might have our independence—the right to make our own decisions about the future of the Six Worlds.

What do you think we would be capable of then?"

Randal was too shocked to try to answer that question. For some reason, he wished that he could hear his mother discussing this with Commander Farre.

"As it is," the Commander went on, "we're putting everything we've got—all our people, all our resources—into fighting for a world that most of us have never seen and never will see."

"But there's loyalty, sir. . . ."

Randal at last found words to protest. The Commander shrugged.

"Ah, yes, loyalty. I was forgetting that." As Randal stared at him, thoroughly confused, he went on, "Go and talk to your cousin, boy. I've had enough of you. Tell the Governor's son that his tutor has been speaking treason."

6

Randal stared at the mathematical problem on his computer screen, and then transferred his gaze to the view from the window. Beyond the edge of the terrace there was nothing but sky. The Governor's house was perched on the side of a mountain. Randal could almost imagine it was flying.

When they had arrived the day before, Randal had been impressed in spite of himself. The house was a single story, designed in a strange shape which followed the contours of the hill. It was built of the local stone so that it still seemed part of the rock. It looked primitive to Randal. He almost expected to find himself drawing water from a well as his history tutor informed him his ancient ancestors had done on Earth. Instead, the house had all the comforts he was used to, but carefully concealed so that nothing spoiled its simplicity.

Two of the Governor's servants were already there: the housekeeper, a large, cheerful woman who sang at her work and could be heard all over the house; and her husband, tall, quiet and withdrawn. As Randal settled in he was sure he could have spent a wonderful holiday here if he had been with his own friends instead of Veryan, and if the threat of work had not been hanging over him.

Now, with the threat a reality, he looked back at the screen. Half-heartedly he tapped a few keys and surveyed the result. Commander Farre, appearing behind him, clicked his tongue disapprovingly.

"Aren't you forgetting that?" he asked, pointing out a symbol in the original equation.

Randal sighed and deleted what he had just done. He knew

but he had no more enthusiasm
here was still an eternity to go

was peering at the screen, brow
kious bursts, interspersed with
mmander Farre left Randal, he
Veryan, checking what he had
two things on the screen with
Randal itched to know what

At length, Commander Farre cleared Veryan's screen and keyed in something else.

"Try that," he suggested. Veryan stared at the screen and then looked up at the Commander, startled. Commander Farre grinned at him. Randal had never seen him smile before. It was attractive if you ignored the disfiguring scar. For the first time Randal thought that this man's approval might be worth working for. The thought was unwelcome and he pushed it away.

Eaten up by curiosity, he walked across the room to get a drink of water from the dispenser. His route took him behind Veryan's seat and he managed a swift glance at his screen. What he saw almost made him stand still and gape. He did not even know the meaning of some of the symbols that by now were snaking across Veryan's screen. And Veryan had said he was weak in computing! Randal felt himself growing hot. Had Veryan just been laughing at him?

The end of the session could not come quickly enough for Randal. As soon as the Commander dismissed them, he went to his room, undressed, and put on swimming things. At the end of the terrace was a natural pool formed by a stream that fell from the rocks above. It had been enlarged for swimming. Randal had tried it out the day before and now he felt it was just what he needed to wash away the miseries of the morning.

Randal took a towel and went out. He met Veryan on the way.

"I'm going for a swim," he said unnecessarily. "Coming?"

Veryan shook his head. "I can't swim."

"I'll teach you, then."

Randal did not know what impulse of friendliness had prompted the offer. Perhaps it was not friendliness at all, but just a twisted way of reminding Veryan that Randal was better than he was at most things. Whatever the reason, the offer was met with another nervous shake of the head.

"Thank you, Randal, but I'm not allowed to."

Randal went on without another word.

He plunged into the pool, enjoying the cold shock of the mountain water. Randal swam vigorously and then floated, staring up into the empty blue above him. He felt at peace with himself for the first time since he had left home. Veryan's voice, when it came, was an intrusion. Randal swam to the side.

"What is it?"

He tossed his hair back, spattering Veryan, who had squatted down to talk to him.

"Lunch is almost ready, Randal." When Randal did not respond, he added timidly, "You should come in."

Irritated, Randal said, "I'll come in when I'm ready."

"But, Randal . . ."

Ignoring him, Randal pushed off again from the side of the pool and propelled himself into the turbulent water where the stream plunged in. By the time he next looked, Veryan had gone.

When Randal thought he had stayed in the pool long enough to make his point, he climbed out and wrapped himself in the towel. He did so quickly, for there was a cool breeze blowing. He padded across the terrace to the door and pressed the button to open it.

Nothing happened. Randal pressed the button again, but the door still did not open. He tried the call signal, but there was no response to that either.

A horrible suspicion started to grow in Randal's mind. Not giving in to it yet, he followed the wall of the house until he came to another door. When that also refused to open, the suspicion settled and refused to be dislodged. Someone had deliberately shut him out.

Commander Farre. Of course. Because he had not come

when he was called, the Commander had chosen this way of punishing him. Setting his teeth on rising anger, Randal wondered what to do. He wondered if there would be an open window he could use to climb in, but he knew that the house must have a central locking system that would be activated at night, or when it was unoccupied. The Commander would have used that. There would be no way for Randal to break in.

As the cold breeze penetrated his damp towel, Randal started to shiver. He was hungry, too, especially since his swim. Slowly he began to work his way around the house.

Before long he came to the window of the dining room. Veryan and the Commander were having lunch. Randal tapped on the window. Veryan saw him and said something to the Commander, obviously pleading. Commander Farre looked round at Randal and gave him a curt nod of acknowledgement before turning back to his meal.

Randal was furious. Added to his cold and hunger now was humiliation. Was he supposed to stand out here, shivering and miserable, until the Commander saw fit to let him in? Perhaps he would even be made to apologize first. *No*, he thought. *I'll stay out here all night before I'll do that.*

He finished his circuit of the house. He had half hoped that he might have persuaded the housekeeper to let him in, but there was no sign of her or her husband. Besides, the Commander would have made sure they had their orders. Standing once more outside the door, hopping from one foot to the other in an attempt to keep warm, Randal began to think.

He could not get back into the house. The longer he stayed out here, the more stupid he would appear. He must somehow show the Commander he was not beaten—that the Commander could not treat him like this and expect to get away with it. Randal did not know what he could do, but he was determined to do something.

He looked around for inspiration. There was nothing on the terrace except some garden furniture. Randal wondered if he could use one of the chairs to break a window, but they were far too light and flimsy. At one end of the terrace was the pool, at the other end sheer rock. A flight of steps led down, but there was nothing at their foot except the landing pad for the flyer. As his eyes fell on the flyer, however, Randal knew what he was going to do.

Briskly he toweled himself off and ran down the steps. If the flyer were locked, his plan would not work. But there would hardly be any need to lock it in such a remote spot. To his relief, the door slid back at his touch and he scrambled into the pilot's seat.

The first thing he did was to switch on the heating and bask in the blast of warmth while he listened for any disturbance from the house. Good. So far no one had seen him. As his shivering died away he examined the controls. He reminded himself of all the procedures he had learned from his father and checked the fuel cell. He was grinning tightly to himself.

When he cut in the engine, the flyer lifted sweetly from the pad. This was the best time of all—to feel the machine quivering under his control, responding delicately, obediently, to summon and put to use all his own skill. He had never flown solo before, but he was fueled by exhilaration. He hardly felt nervous at all.

First of all he steered the flyer down into the valley over part of the route they had followed the day before until he could see in the distance the rooftops of the little town of Carador. It was huddled in the bend of a river where the last of the mountains sank into the plain. Here Randal wheeled and set the controls to gain height. He had no wish to come into contact with possible air traffic above Carador.

He soared toward the mountains. He might fly right over the peak, he thought to himself. Instead he followed the contours of the hill, caught sight of a small mountain lake set like a blue jewel in the gray-green moorland. Randal skimmed the belt of forest below at treetop height. The house was back in sight. And just to make sure, wanting everyone to see him now, he swooped three or four times over the roof before he made his approach to the landing pad.

For the first time he became slightly worried. Landing was the difficult part. And if he were honest, he was not expert at it yet. If he crashed on landing, the whole of his exploit would be ruined. Crashing so badly that he would be killed or injured never entered his head. He made tiny adjustments to the controls, seeming to hear his father's voice calmly repeating the correct procedures. The pad loomed up below him. He cut in the landing jets, felt the flyer brake in the air, and then he was down with a slight jarring as he cut the engines. Not a perfect landing, but nothing to be ashamed of at all. Easily, he swung himself down on to the pad.

Commander Farre was standing at the top of the steps. He said nothing, but waited for Randal to reach the level of the terrace. As Randal approached, he could see the expression of cold fury on his face. Randal's heart lurched, but with exultation as much as with fear. He had done what he set out to do. His mouth tightened as he climbed the last of the steps and stood face to face with the Commander.

Randal lay smoldering on his bed. Over and over again the Commander's blistering rebuke replayed itself in his mind. He had been thoughtless and irresponsible. He could have killed himself or injured himself for life. In flying solo with only a novice license, he had broken the law. If traffic control had found out about his flight, he could have said goodbye to becoming a fleet cadet next year. Perhaps he had better think twice about a fleet career if that was all the respect he had for authority. Randal would have felt less angry if he could have gone on being pleased with himself, but part of his mind was struggling not to admit that Commander Farre was right.

The Commander had finished his lecture by sending Randal to his room. Randal had missed lunch. It looked as if he were going to miss dinner as well. He lay with his face buried in the pillow and seethed, trying to forget how hungry he was. This wasn't the end of it, he promised himself. He would find some way of showing the Commander that he couldn't be treated like a child.

He had locked his door. He was not sure how much later it was when he heard Veryan outside.

"Randal?"

"Go away."

"Randal, please let me in. I've brought you something to eat."

Randal reached out, hit the override button that allowed the door to open, and rolled over to look at Veryan as he came in. His cousin was carrying a tray which he set down carefully on the table beside the bed. There were rolls and cheese, sweet pastries, and a fruit drink. All of Randal's instincts told him to grab a roll and wolf it down, but he made himself hold back.

"The Commander gave in then?" he asked, sneering.

Veryan shook his head.

"No. He doesn't know." He glanced nervously over his shoulder. "Close the door, Randal." Randal touched the button again and the door slid shut.

"I'm surprised you dared," he said.

Veryan said nothing. Randal allowed himself to take a roll, bit into it and chewed deliberately. It was delicious.

After a few mouthfuls he thought to say, ungraciously, "Thank you."

Veryan, who had gone to sit on the window seat, gave him an uncertain, flickering glance.

"Randal, I wish you would apologize," he said.

Randal sat up, scattering crumbs. "Did he send you to say that?"

"No! No. I told you, he doesn't know I'm here. I promise, Randal."

Randal went on eating, considering him. On balance, he believed him, if only because he believed Veryan was too timid to lie to him successfully.

"Why should I?" he asked. "What difference does it make to you?"

"I hate arguments, and—and bad feeling. I hate it when people are angry."

"He's not angry with you," Randal said.

Veryan shrugged awkwardly. He was looking down at his clasped hands, his face almost hidden by the heavy copper hair. When he made no reply, Randal went on, "Anyway, I'm not going to apologize."

Veryan's hands began twisting nervously.

"Randal, if you make him really angry, he could complain to the Governor. Then you might be sent back to Altir. You wouldn't want that, would you?"

He asked the question as if there could only be one possible answer. But Randal, with a sudden inward warmth, realized that being sent back to Altir was exactly what he wanted. If he were there, with the Governor busy, there would be no one to stop him joining Damaris and her friends on the medical project. At worst, he might be sent home. And though his mother would be on Centre, he could live alone in their apartment. The final reckoning he would worry about later.

"You don't know what I want," he said.

He was smiling. Veryan looked up apprehensively. Randal felt marvelous, soaring, in control, just like the moment when the flyer lifted off the pad.

"I'm not going to apologize," he repeated. "And we'll see who wins."

For the next few days, Randal practiced being as difficult as possible. He reported punctually to the workroom, only to sit in front of his screen with the most aggressively stupid expression he could manage. He did no work. The Commander began by trying to encourage him, then became coldly angry. Finally he ignored him. The only thing he did not do was call Altir to report Randal's behavior to the Governor.

That did not discourage Randal from laying his plans. He remembered the mountain lake he had seen on his flight. It would be a good idea, he thought, to get up before everyone else and climb up there and swim. Naturally, he would miss the work session that he should otherwise be attending. By the time the Commander had wasted a good part of the day looking for him, he should be in a good complaining mood.

On the evening before Randal meant to put this plan into operation, he packed his swimming things and sneaked food from the kitchen. He meant to stay out most of the day. When everything was ready, he went back to the sitting room where Veryan and the Commander were playing chess. Randal went and stood over the board, remembering to slouch and look dense.

"Who's winning?"

"He is," the Commander said. "Don't breathe down my neck, lad."

Randal stayed to watch a few moves, but he found it hard to conceal his inward excitement. Soon he moved away to stare out of the window into the darkness. A few minutes later, he heard Veryan say timidly, "Checkmate, sir."

"Well done. Don't sound as if I want to bite you. Randal, do you want a game?"

Randal turned from the window, shaking his head. The chess table was positioned in the glow of a lamp. Veryan's hair shone. He was looking a little less crushed than usual, perhaps pleased by his victory. The Commander was smiling. Randal felt a sudden pang, thinking of the bundle stowed away under his bed. He half-wished he really belonged in friendship with them.

"Can't play, sir."

"Then you should learn. When you're a cadet you'll need something to occupy yourself on the long hauls between planets. Space flight is boring, mostly." Randal stared, disbelieving. "Oh, yes, incredibly boring," the Commander assured him. "Though if you carry on in the way you're going, lad, you're never going to find that out."

Stung, even though he wanted the Commander to accept his stupidity, Randal flushed and did not know what to say. While he was still looking for words, the Commander turned to Veryan.

"You've no ambitions to join the fleet?" he asked. As Veryan shook his head, the Commander's voice grew harder as he went on, "What are you going to do, then?"

Veryan flushed uncomfortably.

"I don't know, sir. I've always thought . . . because they say I wouldn't be strong enough, and I've never—" He stammered into an unhappy silence. The Commander watched him, mouth set uncompromisingly, his scar suddenly looking very prominent.

"You're a mathematician. You do realize that, don't you?"

Veryan's eyes widened. "No, sir."

"Then it's time you did. You've a God-given talent and it will be criminal if you don't study."

"But how can I?"

The Commander leaned forward over the chess table, tipping over several pieces.

"That's the question you should be asking. Seriously asking. There must be a way."

Veryan was looking down. He had raised one hand to his lips. He looked as if he might burst into tears. His voice almost inaudible, he murmured, "Not for me, sir."

The Commander brought his hand down flat on the table.

"Rubbish! If you—"

He broke off as if he were really looking at Veryan for the first time and realizing the state he was in.

"Very well," he said coldly. "Be spineless, if that's what you prefer. It's your affair, not mine. And as for you . . ." He swung around on Randal who had been listening, fascinated. "You're someone else who's wasting a God-given talent. Don't think I believe you're as stupid as you pretend to be."

He thrust his chair back and stood up. One or two chess pieces rolled onto the floor.

"What I ever did," he said, "to deserve being in charge of a pair of spoiled brats like you, I can't imagine." Without waiting for a reply, he limped rapidly out of the room.

While Veryan bent and groped blindly after the chess pieces, Randal stared after the Commander. He was furious. Being identified with Veryan was only part of it. There was something about the Commander's cold dismissiveness, as if he had assessed Randal and found nothing at all admirable in him. Those seemingly deliberate actions by the Commander made Randal want to give up all his plans and work as hard as he could to prove him wrong.

He thrust the impulse away from him. He would not let the Commander win. Besides, he wanted to go back to Altir, and the only way to get there was for the Governor to remove him. Uncontrollable. A bad influence on Veryan. The phrases went through Randal's head as he prepared for bed that night. They were still there when he woke early the next morning. Very quietly, without disturbing anyone, he slid out of the house and took the path up into the hills.

8

Do I assume, Randal, that you're out to make life as difficult as possible for everyone?" the Commander asked, every word savagely bitten off. "If so, tell me and I'll act accordingly."

Randal did not reply. He stood in the sitting room, fixed his eyes on the opposite wall, and composed his face into the expression his own father called "dumb insolence."

He was tired, filthy, and disheveled from his expedition up to the lake, but he felt marvelous. He had spent a whole day in complete freedom, and after the first hour or so had given very little thought to Veryan or the Commander or what he would have to face when he got back.

The light of a brilliant sunset washed into the room, kindling Veryan's hair to flame. Veryan was curled up in one of the deep armchairs, a tight knot of apprehension, eyes wide and wretched as he listened in silence to the Commander's rebuke.

"If you think," the Commander went on, "that this sort of thing is either clever or amusing, you can think again. It is mindless, immature defiance. I don't propose to waste any more time arguing with you. Go to your room. You may join us again when you have decided to behave like a reasonable adult."

He turned away. Veryan murmured, "Oh, please . . ."

Halfway to the door the Commander swung around toward him. "I don't know which is worse—Randal trying to demonstrate just how obnoxious it's possible to be, or you with your perpetual whining. Be quiet."

He left the room without giving Veryan a chance to defend himself.

"He doesn't know what he wants," Randal said. "You're so good it hurts, and he still doesn't like you."

Veryan looked up at him from the depths of the chair, gave a tiny shrug, and turned his head away. Randal heaved an elaborate sigh.

"I suppose I'd better do as I'm told."

The day's exploit had been an open declaration of war. Randal continued his campaign by slipping away whenever he felt like it, exploring his surroundings. He was feeling happier with every day that passed, to be out on his own with no one to tell him what to do.

He varied his plan by turning up now and then in the workroom, though by now he had given up all pretense of actually working. While he was sitting doing nothing, he could not help noticing how impatient the Commander had become with Veryan.

"You're not trying!" the Commander snapped at him one morning a few days after Randal's expedition to the lake. Veryan raised anxious eyes to him.

"Truly, sir, I—"

"You've spent all your life pretending to be incapable, and now it's probably too late to be anything else."

There was a scathing contempt in his voice. Randal heard a tiny gasp of protest from Veryan, instantly stifled. Instead of speaking, he leaned toward the screen, earnestly scanning the problem.

"Don't overexert yourself!" the Commander taunted.

For a few seconds Veryan did not move. Then, with a half sob, he slammed his hand down on the keyboard and fled from the room. Randal stared after him, forgetting for a minute to slump in his chair and look uninterested. Warily, he stole a glance at the Commander. The man was actually smiling—a faint, satisfied curl of the mouth, the scar lifting it crookedly. Briefly Randal regretted not being Veryan's friend. Even so, it was hard to bite back a protest.

Ten minutes later Veryan returned, red-eyed and subdued.

"I'm sorry, sir," he said to the Commander. "Will you key the problem in again, please? I'll try harder this time."

The Commander, tight-mouthed and unforgiving, moved over to his screen to do as he asked. Randal's impulse of sympathy faded. Apologizing so meekly was just like Veryan!

The incident stung Randal into putting the next phase of his plan into operation. He was familiar by now with most of the paths over the hills and through the forest within a half day's walk from the house. The mountainside lake had been the limit of his exploration. Now Randal wanted to go farther—to climb the nearest peak.

He had been working out his route for some days and had even consulted maps that he found on the bookshelves of the house. He thought he had discovered the best way—no actual climbing, just a hard scramble. It would take all day. No one would know where he was. And if he did not return until after dark, the Commander might just be goaded into getting rid of him.

Satisfied with his plans, he waited until he thought everyone would be asleep and then slid into the kitchen to pack his supplies for the next day. He was cutting bread when a slight sound behind him made him turn. His breath came short for a second as he imagined it was the housekeeper, or even the Commander. But then he relaxed. It was only Veryan.

"What do you want?" he asked.

Veryan kept his enormous eyes fixed on Randal as he crossed the room and started to draw fruit juice into a glass from the dispenser.

"I wanted a drink," he said.

He was wearing the blue silk dressing gown. His hair was disheveled, as if he had been to bed and gotten up again. The skin around his eyes looked bruised, and his head drooped as if it were too heavy for him to hold up. Randal wondered what would happen if Veryan became really ill so far from a medical center.

Veryan stood sipping the fruit juice and watching Randal.

"You're going out again tomorrow," he said.

"So?" Randal finished cutting the bread and started poking

around for sandwich fillings. "I suppose you're going to tell the Commander."

Veryan's eyes, huge and reproachful, never left Randal, making him feel uneasy.

"You know I won't," Veryan said. Hesitantly, he added, "Randal, what's the matter? Why are you doing this?"

Randal almost told him to mind his own business. Instead, he found himself answering.

"I'm not going to let him win." He did not trust Veryan enough to tell him what his real purpose was, so he went on. "What are you worrying about? He's not exactly nice to you, is he?"

Veryan flinched a little. Drearily, he said, "It doesn't matter. He won't stay very long. No one ever does."

"He can't leave soon enough for me," Randal said.

Rapidly he began putting his sandwiches together, wishing that Veryan would finish his drink and leave. Instead, Veryan went on watching him.

"Where do you go?" he asked.

"Up the mountain," Randal replied. "Tomorrow I'm going to climb the peak." Unnerved by Veryan's scrutiny, he added, "Why are you staring at me? Why can't you leave me alone?"

He half expected that his harshness would drive Veryan away. But Veryan only drew a shaken breath and said, "I'm sorry, Randal. When . . . when I heard you were coming, I hoped we might be friends."

He spoke without any accusation or bitterness, only a deep regret. Randal's impatience spilled over.

"Friends? Why do you think I would want to be your friend? You never do anything, except droop around the place as if you're going to faint at any minute. We can't share anything. I've other friends I'd rather be with, and I could be if I hadn't been forced out here into the back of nowhere!"

He was not quite aware of how cruel the words sounded until they were out. Veryan had gone white, but he never moved. They gazed at each other for a moment. In the end it was Randal who snatched up his provisions and fled from the kitchen.

Randal slept poorly that night. He told himself it was excitement about the next day's expedition. He was out of bed with the first gray light of dawn. The sky was clouded, threatening rain. For half a minute Randal wondered whether to abandon his scheme. He pushed the idea firmly to the back of his mind. He would not let Veryan or the Commander think he was giving in. But before he left his room he pushed a lightweight raincoat into the top of his knapsack.

Once he was away from the house, the sky seemed to brighten though the clouds did not clear. He was following the course of the stream that fed the pool.

By and by the day grew warmer. By the time Randal reached the forest, he was grateful for the cool shade found under the trees.

The path led upwards quite steeply beside the water. It was damp and the air was filled with a strong scent of pine. Small stones skittered away under his feet. He began to relax and forget the problems behind him. He looked forward to climbing the peak ahead.

It was still early in the morning when he stopped to rest in a favorite spot he had discovered on his first expedition. The stream spilled into a small pool where dragonflies, metallic blue and green, hovered over the water. A small, flat piece of ground, covered with grass fine as hair growing through a mat of pine needles, projected over the stream. Through a gap in the trees, Randal could see sky and distant hills. He lay down to rest on the patch of earth, panting heavily.

As the sound of his own breathing returned to normal, he became aware of other sounds—sounds that were not the splash of the stream or the subdued rustle of the trees: the alarm call of a bird further down the slope, the rattling of loose stones on the path. Randal sat up.

On all of his wanderings he had never met anyone else. The hills were deserted. But he was convinced now that someone was coming up the path after him, still hidden by the trees and undergrowth that fringed the stream. He felt a tightness in his throat, a brief anticipation of danger. Almost at once it vanished as his unknown follower appeared around a bend in the path. Randal's fear was swallowed up in irritation as he watched the small figure toiling up the path, as yet unconscious that he was there. It was Veryan.

9

Randal stayed where he was and waited in silence until Veryan had struggled up to the level of the pool. His cousin's eyes were on the ground as he chose his footholds carefully on the steep path.

When only a few yards separated them, Randal said, "What do you think you're doing?"

Veryan's head jerked up. He was flushed. His chest heaved as he fought for breath. He stared at Randal but said nothing. Randal wondered if he could manage to speak. He himself said nothing more until Veryan had scrambled up the last few feet and collapsed on the grass at his side. Then he asked, "Well?"

For at least a minute, Veryan could not get his breath. At last, he gasped out, "I want to climb the mountain."

"You?" Randal was incredulous. "What for?"

An expression of pure obstinacy settled on Veryan's face. It was so unlike what Randal had come to expect of him that he was taken aback.

"To show you I can," Veryan said.

He stretched out flat on the ground. Randal looked down at him. He was wearing light clothes and shoes that were not really suitable for climbing. There was a smear of mud down one side, showing that he had fallen at least once.

"You're out of your mind," Randal said. "You'll never get up there."

He was surprised that Veryan had even gotten this far. His anger rising, he began tearing at the grass. "You can't come with me," he said. "I don't want you. I want to be on my own."

CHAPTER 9

Veryan half sat up. Randal almost flinched at the blaze in his eyes.

"I haven't asked to come with you." His voice was low, vibrant with bitterness. "I thought you would be well ahead by now. I haven't asked anything from you! But I'm sick of being left behind and sneered at and treated as if . . ."

He broke off, a hand pressed to his mouth. Randal was quite prepared for him to burst into tears.

The struggle was plain, but after a moment Veryan recovered himself and said quietly, "I'm going to do it. You can't stop me."

Sitting erect now, he curled his arms around his knees and gazed out across the pool as if he were trying to pretend Randal was not there.

Uneasily, Randal said, "You'll be out all day, you know."

Veryan gave a curt nod toward a small knapsack that he had dropped on the grass beside him. "I brought some food."

Taking the nod as invitation, Randal lifted the flap of the knapsack and peered inside. A few rolls, some fruit, a plastic water bottle. Of course, Veryan had watched what he had brought for himself.

"You don't know the way," he said.

"There's a path."

"Yes, but . . ."

Once beyond the lake, Randal did not know the way himself. The path would probably die out long before it reached the summit. He had a cold feeling in his stomach at the thought of his cousin wandering around helplessly lost on the hillside.

"You'll have to go back," he said.

Veryan's head whipped round toward him.

"I won't! You can't make me!"

Furious with him, Randal sprang to his feet. "All right, kill yourself! Because that's what's going to happen."

He snatched up his own knapsack and strode across the grass to where the path began its upward winding once more. Here he turned back to look at Veryan. His eyes met a silent, mutinous stare.

"Don't expect me to help you," Randal said, and went on up the path.

Not far beyond his resting place, the trees began to thin out and give way to thornbushes and scrub on the side of the mountain. Soon Randal came to the place where the path divided. One branch led to the lake, the other up toward the peak. Randal hesitated, wondering whether he ought to leave some sort of marker to tell Veryan which path to take. But he was still annoyed.

"It's obvious, isn't it?" he asked himself. "This way goes up. If he's too stupid to see it . . . Anyway, he's probably given up by now."

He still paused, glancing back down the steep slope he had just climbed. The trees were a dark barrier below him. But he thought he saw, just for an instant, a flash of white that might have been Veryan's shirt. His cousin was still following. With an angry jerk of the head Randal moved on again.

Usually there was a fresh breeze on the moorland, but today the air was still, almost thick. Randal found his breath coming in long, painful gasps. He paused, looking up at the sky. The clouds had grown darker, heavier, and so low that he could not see the peak any longer. In the distance, he heard a faint mutter of thunder.

Now he had another reason to hesitate. So far he had known only good weather on his expeditions. He did not like the idea of being caught out on the mountain in a storm. He began to look around for shelter. There were a few clusters of rock close by, none of them more than a windbreak. The forest would be better, but that meant going a long way down.

As Randal stood still, a light breeze sprang up, bending the grasses, making him shiver. It felt strange, for a moment ago he had been sweating from the exertion of climbing. Then thunder crashed out over his head and rain drilled down from the sky. Hardly thinking now, Randal headed downward, skidding and sliding on the path that had suddenly changed into a river of mud. Not until then did he remember Veryan.

He looked for his cousin, calling out to him, but his cries were drowned by the almost perpetual rumble of thunder. He could see no more than a few yards through the solid cascade of rain. By the time he reached the fork in the path, he had not found Veryan, though he did not think they could have missed each other.

Randal stood panting, rain streaming down his face, peering through the curtain of water.

"Veryan! Veryan!" he shouted. He could hear no reply. Surely even Veryan would have reached this place by now. So what if he had taken the path to the lake?

A jolt of pure terror took Randal's breath away. The path to the lake led on to a bluff that was twenty feet or more above the water. You had to follow the shore for some time before there was a safe way down. But Veryan had never been there before and in this rain he might miss the edge of the bluff. And Veryan could not swim. . . .

Randal had not put words to all that in his mind before he was racing down the path. Lightning veined the sky. The thunder followed it as if the world were splitting apart. Randal called out again, but any reply would have been swamped by the rain and his own sobbing breath.

Just before it reached the lake, the path passed between rocks that jutted out just up above Randal's head. Water gurgled around his ankles. Then he came out into the open space at the head of the bluff and saw in front of him something white. An arm was raised, someone was struggling. . . .

"Hold on!" he cried.

Veryan had fallen at the very edge and was trying to cling to soil and turf that crumbled away under his hands. It was now loosened and dissolved by the pelting rain. Randal flung himself to his knees, grabbed Veryan's arm and hauled him upwards. Veryan clutched at him. For a moment they hung poised on the edge, the waters of the mountain lake lapping below. Then they crouched on the grass, clinging to each other. Randal could feel Veryan sobbing and shaking, and just then he was not much better himself. He gasped for air that was half water, more than anything relieved that he was not guilty of leaving Veryan to serious injury or worse.

When he had himself under control again, Randal slid an arm around Veryan and pulled him to his feet. Beside the path not far away was an overhanging rock, cut away deeply enough underneath to offer some shelter. Randal urged Veryan toward it, half-carrying him. He let Veryan slip to the ground with his back against the rock wall.

Veryan's shirt was torn and plastered with mud. Randal stripped it off. He took a towel from his knapsack and rubbed Veryan briskly with it. Then Randal made him put on the spare sweater he was carrying and his raincoat. They were both too big for Veryan, but they were warm. Veryan's shivering gradually died away. As he revived, he fixed his disturbingly intense gaze on Randal, his eyes enormous.

"Thank you," he murmured. And then, "I'm sorry, Randal."

"There's nothing to be sorry for," Randal replied. "If it comes to that, I'm sorry, too. I should have stayed with you."

Veryan said nothing. Randal, uneasy, watched the rain billowing across the surface of the lake. Now and again it swept into their shelter, but mostly they stayed dry. The first force of the storm was dying away. To Randal's surprise, it had not lasted very long.

Soon the rain lessened and the sky began to clear. Randal could make out the opposite shore of the lake. Veryan was leaning back against the rock wall, his eyes closed. He looked white, exhausted.

"Do you want something to eat?" Randal asked. He felt hungry now that the danger was over. Veryan half awoke and looked vaguely around him.

"I've lost my knapsack somewhere."

"Have some of mine, then."

He handed Veryan one of the sandwiches that had been slapped together so quickly the night before. He remembered what he had said to Veryan then in the kitchen. No wonder his cousin had been goaded into proving himself.

All this is my fault, Randal thought.

Another voice seemed to answer him, "So what are you going to do about it?"

While they ate, the rain stopped and the sky cleared. The dark clouds were drawing off to the west while overhead all was clear blue. The sun began to draw up a mist from the rain-soaked ground. The grass sparkled. Randal ventured out from their shelter.

"We might as well move," he said. "Are you all right?"

Veryan nodded silently. He watched while Randal repacked his knapsack and followed him back along the path. At the edge of the bluff, Randal retrieved Veryan's knapsack that was hanging over the edge. Its strap was broken and was snagged on a root. He handed it to Veryan. His cousin murmured something with a nervous, flickering glance at him. He seemed about to say something else when he lapsed into silence.

When they came to the place where the paths divided, Randal pointed.

"You took the wrong turn," he explained. "That's the way to the peak."

"I see."

Veryan's voice was flat. Slowly and reluctantly with his head bowed, he began walking down the path back toward the edge of the forest.

"Where are you going?" Randal asked. Veryan did not stop or look at him.

"Home."

It was the same flat voice, hopeless, defeated. Randal felt himself beginning to smile. A glorious sense of challenge was sweeping over him, and this time it was something he had no reason at all to be ashamed of.

"Why?" he asked. "I thought you wanted to climb the mountain."

10

eryan stopped and turned. His face was transformed with an incredulous hope.

"Randal, I . . . I can't," he said.

"Why not?" He waited, grinning, while Veryan tried to think of a good reason. At last he said, "Come on. We'll do it together."

Hesitantly, Veryan took a step back toward him.

"Do you really think? . . ."

"Yes, of course I really think!" He held out a hand. "Veryan, if you got this far, you can do the rest. Come on." He laughed. "You know, we're going to get a really monumental telling-off from the Commander. We might as well make it worthwhile!"

Suddenly Veryan was laughing too, walking beside him up the path. The peak, now towering above their heads, did not seem so far away.

The path became less steep, tracking back and forth across the hills. At last, as Randal had expected, it gave out altogether. Looking back, they could see the dark mass of the forest. Beyond it all was blue and misty.

The day grew warmer still. Veryan had taken off Randal's raincoat, and in the borrowed sweater he was flushed with the heat. He looked the exact opposite of the neat, subdued creature Randal had known until now. Though Randal was conscious of slowing his own pace to match Veryan's, conscious too that Veryan was finding the climb difficult, his cousin did not complain. And it was Randal who suggested when they should stop and rest.

As they approached the summit they saw a rock wall rising sheer in front of them. Beyond it was only sky. Up here it was colder, though the sun still shone. They sheltered from the stiff breeze in the niche of the wall and shared some food. Randal examined the rocks.

"We have to get up there. . . ."

"Randal, I don't think I can."

Randal was struck by the difference in Veryan's tone. It was not frightened or shrinking, but just a matter-of-fact acceptance of his own limitations.

Randal grinned at him. "Don't you believe it."

He returned to his scrutiny of the wall. It was not as sheer as it had appeared from a distance. There were cracks in the rock, deep enough for grass and heather to grow there, and even the occasional straggling shrub. In places the rock had fallen away.

"If you used that heap of rock as a step," Randal thought, doing it almost as soon as he thought of it, "and then that crack as a foothold . . . and held on to that bush . . . and another step there—you would be up!"

Sucking a scratched hand, he stood on the flat top of the rock wall and stared.

"Veryan!" he called. "You have to come up here!"

He knelt on the edge, above Veryan who stood looking doubtfully at the rock face.

"Come on! You saw the way I did it."

Still uncertain, Veryan climbed to the top of the heap of rock, but his foot slipped in the crack and he slid down again. Randal could see that it was harder for him because the foot and handholds that even Randal had needed to stretch for were almost out of his reach. He tried again. This time he got as far as grabbing the bush and he hung there, helpless.

"Randal, I'm stuck!"

"No, you're not. Look . . . there . . . that knob of rock."

Veryan made a desperate lunge and Randal, lying flat, reached down and managed to get a grip on his wrist. Feet scrabbling, Veryan forced himself upward and Randal hauled him over the edge where he lay gasping.

"Now," Randal said when he had given him a minute to recover, "get up and look at this."

He pulled Veryan to his feet. Buffeted by the wind, they stood together and gazed. On the other side of the ridge, slopes and walls and precipices of rock fell away into air. They looked down and saw birds flying below them. They stood at the head of a vast, horseshoe-shaped valley. Far in the distance they caught the glint of a winding river before all was lost in mist. Veryan laughed incredulously.

"Randal, we can see the whole world!"

He was clutching at Randal as if he thought the wind would carry him off his feet. But he was not afraid. He was exultant, even transformed.

"You did it!" Randal said.

Suddenly he turned Veryan toward him, gripping his shoulders and looking down into the excited face.

"Veryan, if you can do this, you can do other things. You don't have to stop now."

He could see understanding dawn in Veryan's face, the grasping of possibilities that until now he had always dismissed.

"Randal, do you really think? . . ."

"You keep asking me that. Yes, I do—provided you're not blown off this rock. Let's get down."

With a last glance at the panorama spread out in front of them, they retreated to the edge of the rock wall they had climbed. Randal went first, and guided Veryan down. At the foot they rested before beginning the descent. All the way down, Veryan was quiet. Randal kept alert to steady him if he stumbled. But apart from that he left him with his own thoughts.

They reached the fork in the path before Randal realized something he should have thought about long before. The sun was close to setting. Already it had dipped below the tops of the forest trees, casting a black swath of shadow toward them. He had been so fascinated by the change in Veryan that he had never thought about how time was passing.

He halted only for a second and then grasped Veryan's wrist, urging him on faster.

"What's the matter?" Veryan asked.

"It's getting late," Randal replied. "We have to hurry. Let me help you."

The path was much steeper now and Veryan had grown desperately tired. He needed Randal's hand to steady him. By the time they reached the edge of the forest, Randal knew that trying to hurry was no use. Already the sunlight had gone and a gray evening was closing around them. Under the trees night was gathering.

Randal stopped and put Veryan gently down on a rock beside the path.

"Veryan, listen. . . ."

His cousin looked up at him, gasping for breath after the rapid descent of the mountainside. He was puzzled by Randal's manner, but undismayed.

"Veryan," Randal went on, "it's getting dark. It's my fault. The storm held us up and I didn't realize what time it was. We won't be able to get back. We'll have to spend the night here."

Veryan gazed around, still confused.

"Here?"

"It's dangerous to go on in the dark," Randal explained patiently. "One of us might slip and be hurt. We'll have to sleep out, but don't worry. It won't be . . ."

"Yes, I can see that," Veryan interrupted. "Only, Randal, I'm sure you know best, but do we have to stay here? Wouldn't it be more sheltered under the trees?"

"Well, of course. I didn't mean—" Randal broke off, exploding into laughter. "Veryan, I don't know what's gotten into you! I thought you would be scared stiff."

"Should I be?" There was something mischievous about the look he was giving Randal. "Randal, I've climbed the mountain. I think I can do anything! Well," he admitted with an impish smile, "almost. I'm not afraid of sleeping out. Shouldn't we go on before it gets any darker?"

Feeling thoroughly put in his place, Randal led the way down the slope and under the trees, half turning to give a hand to Veryan. Already he had to peer down at his feet to make sure of the footholds.

"You know," he said, "the Commander is going to be furious."

There was a thoughtful pause. Then Veryan replied, "I don't care."

Eventually they came to the spit of ground beside the pool where Randal had first seen Veryan following him up the path. Now twilight was thickening to dark. It was dangerous to go on any further. Randal and Veryan sank down beside the stream and sat listening to the soft plash of the water into the pool. It was the only sound in the forest vastness.

They shared the remains of Randal's sandwiches. There was a little fruit left which they could keep for breakfast. They drank at the stream and Randal refilled the water bottles. When he had finished, he turned back to Veryan to see that his cousin was kneeling, his head bent. Randal almost asked him if he were feeling ill, but he stopped himself in time as he realized that Veryan must be praying. He had an impulse to kneel beside him, but before he could decide Veryan looked up. His face was a pale blur in the darkness and his expression faintly apologetic.

Half wishing he had made his mind up a little faster, Randal groped for his knapsack and fished out the raincoat. He gave it to Veryan.

"You'd better put that on again," he said. "It'll be colder than you think."

"Thank you." Veryan took it and wriggled into it. "I'll be all right," he promised. His voice was muffled by the folds of fabric. "Good night, Randal."

"Good night."

Almost instinctively Veryan curled up in a sheltered hollow at the foot of a tree. Feeling too restless to settle right away, Randal sat beside him, listening as he shifted uncomfortably for a few moments. Then he grew still. If Randal bent close to him he could hear his quiet breathing. Satisfied and suddenly weary beyond description, he lay down at Veryan's side and slept.

Sunlight woke him. Shafts of it, golden and shimmering, slanted down through the trees. Birds were singing. Feeling cramped and stale, Randal sat up, untangled himself from a branch he had unaccountably been sleeping on, and brushed pine needles off himself. He rose, stretched, and then bent over the stream to drink and splash himself in the icy water.

After that he felt better, but ravenously hungry. Veryan was still sleeping. Randal could not bear to wait for breakfast. He examined their provisions and scrupulously divided the remaining fruit along with a single, squashed roll that had escaped notice in the darkness.

As he ate his share, he thought.

There was no way to hide that they had not come home the night before. There was going to be a scolding of quite stupendous proportions. Only the day before Randal would have relished it. Now he was afraid that he might at last get what he had been aiming for and be packed off back to Altir. He admitted to himself that he did not want to go. He wanted to stay and get to know Veryan better.

As if roused by his thoughts, his cousin sat up, rubbing sleep from his eyes.

"Randal—I can't move!"

Randal grinned at him. "You're just stiff," he said unsympathetically. "It'll wear off. Have a wash in the stream."

Veryan crawled across to the bank and splashed water in his face. Randal pushed his share of the food across to him. Veryan gave it a look of disgust. He nibbled at the crust of the roll and suddenly began to eat hungrily.

"Do you think," he asked Randal between mouthfuls, "that we could come up here and camp properly—with sleeping bags?"

When they set out, Randal did not force the pace. There was no point in hurrying and the woods were very pleasant. Veryan began asking him the names of trees and plants. Randal was embarrassed to find that more often than not he did not know.

"There might be a book at the house," Veryan said.

The sun was rising toward midday when they finally broke out of the forest and the house came in sight below. Veryan stopped and reached out to grip Randal's arm.

"Look!"

For a minute Randal did not understand what he meant. The

house seemed just the same—gray and comfortable in its niche in the rock. Then he realized that on the landing pad a second flyer was drawn up beside the first. It looked just the same except that it had some kind of official insignia on its wings.

"What's that?" Randal asked.

Veryan turned to look at him. His eyes were wide and apprehensive again.

"It's one of the Altir fleet," he said. "The Governor must have come to see us."

No one appeared to greet Randal and Veryan as they clambered down the last stretches of the slope behind the house. Everything was ominously silent. As he followed Veryan indoors, Randal found himself walking softly, as if they might be able to slip inside without being noticed.

In the passage Veryan paused and looked up at him, with the same wide-eyed, apprehensive gaze. Randal shrugged.

"Nothing we can do," he said.

Veryan touched the door release of the sitting room. As the door slid back, Randal heard the Governor's voice, pitched on a note of icy displeasure.

"... totally fail to understand how such criminal negligence ..."

Randal could see him over Veryan's shoulder. He was standing with his back to them, lecturing the Commander, who stood at attention. His face was frozen, eyes fixed on nothing. Then at the sound of the door, the Governor broke off what he was saying and swung around. Randal saw relief leap into the Commander's face.

"Veryan . . . Randal. . . ." For a few seconds the Governor sounded completely at a loss. It was a human reaction which he banished almost at once. "May I ask where you have been?"

"We climbed the mountain, sir," Veryan replied. "I climbed it with Randal. And I wasn't afraid, or tired—or only a little— but then we were too late to . . ."

His pride in his own achievement was at war with nervousness, and he stumbled to a halt under the Governor's cold eyes.

"Veryan," the Governor said, "I thought that your mother

and I had made you understand the way you must live. No one is more sorry than I am that you cannot do the same things as other young people of your age. But you must learn to accept that you are not strong enough for such activities as . . . " contempt dripped from his tongue, ". . . mountain-climbing. Indeed, I believe—"

"But he is strong enough!" Randal interrupted. "You can see he is."

The Governor turned a look of dislike on him.

"I can see no such thing. All that I see is that he will now face such a breakdown in his health that he will lose the little progress he has made. Veryan, go to bed at once."

Veryan had gone white. He looked as if he were going to be sick. Very briefly a spark lit in his eyes as if he might defy the Governor's order. But it soon faded and he turned submissively to go. At the door he turned back.

"I'm sorry, sir," he said. "Please don't blame Randal. It wasn't his idea. It was mine."

He went out. Randal heard his footsteps dragging along the passage toward his room. Furiously angry, he faced the Governor. "Can't you see what you're doing?" he asked. "He could be—"

"Be quiet," the Governor interrupted. "You have done enough damage. Without your influence this would never have happened. You're fortunate that my affairs don't allow me to take you back to Altir with me. And I understand your mother is not available to take responsibility for you. If she were, you would find yourself on the next shuttle. Now go to your room."

There were whole volumes that Randal could have spoken, but it was plain that none of them would be of the slightest use. He turned to go.

Before the door hissed shut he heard the Governor say, "As for you, Commander, you're dismissed from your post."

Randal did not try to hear what else he might have to say. He moved quietly along the passage, hoping the Governor would not realize that he was not going to his own room, but to Veryan's.

The door was standing open. Veryan had flung himself down on the bed and he was sobbing slowly, hopelessly, clutching his pillow.

Randal gazed at him for a moment, not knowing what to do. Awkwardly he said, "Veryan, don't . . ."

Veryan seemed not to hear him. Randal was moving forward when there was a footstep behind him. Commander Farre brushed past him into the room.

"Veryan!" The voice was domineering. "Veryan, stop it."

When the desperate sobbing still continued, the Commander limped across to the bed and sat down. He grasped Veryan's shoulder and forced him to sit up.

"Stop that, Veryan."

Randal took a step forward. "Leave him alone!"

Still gripping Veryan's shoulder, the Commander jerked round to face Randal.

"Don't be so stupid! He doesn't want pampering. Can't you see that? You of all people? Go and get him some water—and close that door or we'll have the Governor down on us."

Taken aback, Randal obeyed almost without realizing it. When he came back with the water, Veryan was gasping for breath, trying to control his sobs. He was leaning against the Commander who had an arm around his shoulders. The Commander took the glass with a nod of thanks to Randal.

"Drink this and pull yourself together," he said to Veryan. "We have to decide what to do, and I haven't much time."

"What do you mean?" Randal asked.

"I mean, what happens now?" It was Veryan he was speaking to. "Are you just going back to where you were before?"

Veryan looked up at him uncertainly and gulped down some of the water. "The Governor says I'm going to be ill."

"And are you?" That seemed a strange question to Randal, but Veryan took it seriously.

"I—I don't know."

"Do you think the person who climbed the mountain and spent the night out of doors without looking more than . . . well, slightly disreputable—" He was smiling now and Randal found that he had to revise rapidly all the opinions he had formed about the Commander. "Do you think that he's going to take to his bed and be ill?"

Veryan stared at him and then straightened suddenly, brushing at the traces of his tears.

"No," he said.

"Good."

"Just a minute," Randal said, feeling thoroughly bewildered. "Are you saying that you're pleased with us? I thought you were going to be furious!"

"Give me strength!" The Commander covered his eyes with one hand. "What do you think I've been playing at since we came here, if not trying to prod Veryan into standing up for himself? I wanted to make him so angry with me that he would do something—anything—to prove me wrong about him. In which I had your help, may I say, though I don't think that was quite what you had in mind."

His eyes glinted at Randal. He was half-laughing, enjoying their astonishment.

"You mean you wanted me to disobey you?" Veryan asked.

"Very much. I thought I had you the day you dashed out of the workroom, but then you came back and apologized. That was a big disappointment."

Bewildered, Veryan shook his head.

"I don't understand, sir. I thought you would be angry. The Governor has always said—"

"Do as you're told and don't presume to question those in authority?" The Commander's tones were scathing. "Veryan, that's all very well for children, but there comes a time when you have to take responsibility for yourself. Only God deserves our complete obedience. Anyone else can make a mistake and . . ."

"You must have obeyed orders when you were in the fleet, sir," Randal pointed out.

"Yes. And toward the end, I was obeying orders I didn't really agree with. But what could I do? We were at war. There was no way of getting out. This . . . " he touched his scar, ". . . was a blessing in many ways."

For a moment he remained silent, fingering the puckered tissue at the side of his mouth. His eyes were dark with memory. Then he shook his head as if to clear it.

"Never mind that," he said. "What you have to realize, Veryan, is that the Governor is wrong about you. Even if he is your father. . . ."

"He's not my father!"

Suddenly, Veryan was on fire with indignation. Randal gaped at him.

"Randal, you must know!" Veryan said. "Your mother must have told you. My real father was a fleet doctor and his ship was lost—oh, years ago when I was very young. I think that was when I first started to be ill. This was his," he explained, reaching out to the Bible on the table by the bed. "He left it behind when he went on his last voyage. Afterwards my mother married the Governor." His face set with the obstinate expression Randal had seen before. "I've always obeyed him, but I won't call him 'father.' "

He sighed wearily and leaned against the Commander's shoulder. Thinking it over, Randal vaguely recalled his mother saying something about all this, but at the time it had not seemed important.

"What happens now?" he asked.

"I don't know," the Commander said. "You would choose to stage your rebellion just at the very time the Governor came to visit. I was hoping he would know nothing about all this until I'd had more time with you. Veryan, I could have coached you until you were ready to apply for a university place, but now . . ."

"What do you mean?" Veryan asked. "Aren't you going to stay?" The Commander shook his head.

"The Governor has dismissed me. He thinks I'm packing now. I have to go back to Altir with him today."

For a moment Randal thought that Veryan would give way to tears again.

"Everyone goes away," he said bitterly.

"But I don't want to," the Commander said. "And Randal is staying—even if he did do his best to get sent home." His smile surfaced again. "Don't think I didn't know!"

Randal tried scowling but found he had to laugh instead.

"All right," he said. "You had it all planned, didn't you, sir? What do you want me to do now?"

For a few days after the Governor left, Randal and Veryan were alone in the house except for the housekeeper and her husband, who paid no attention to what they did. The Governor had promised to find a tutor for them who was really capable of keeping them in order. But until he arrived, there was no one to tell them what to do.

In the mornings they worked on assignments the Commander had already programmed into the computer. In the afternoons they went exploring again into the hills. Randal began to teach Veryan to swim in the pool on the terrace. In the evenings Veryan taught Randal to play chess.

On the third evening after supper, Randal was staring at the chess pieces. He was convinced there must be some clever move he could make to get himself out of trouble, but he had no idea at all of what it might be.

"You know," he said, "there's something bothering me."

Veryan was seated at the other side of the board, his chin resting on cupped hands.

"My queen," he suggested.

"No. Your father. I mean, the Governor. He went storming out of here the other day, threatening to send us some sort of prison warden. But no one's arrived. Not even a radio call."

Veryan shrugged. "It doesn't bother me."

Randal grinned at him. He found his new and independent cousin very engaging.

"But listen. Here you are, shut up with no one to look after you except a bad character like me. I thought the Governor would have sent someone out the next day."

Veryan returned the grin. "Perhaps he couldn't find anyone prepared to take on a bad character like you."

"Well, I think we ought to do something," Randal said. "Call him, perhaps." He caught the beginnings of Veryan's obstinate look. "If no one comes tomorrow," he added.

Veryan hesitated, and then said, "All right. I was going to call the Commander, anyway. We'll do it tomorrow evening."

The next day no one came, and there was still no word from the Governor. Even Veryan was becoming anxious. That evening they went to the workroom and Veryan keyed in the radio code for his home in Altir.

Instead of the screen clearing as the connection was made, or the sound of an engaged signal, a loud crackling noise came from the radio. The screen flashed silver in jagged bursts of light.

"What's wrong with it?" Veryan asked. "Randal, do you know?"

"No. Try the Commander."

Veryan keyed in the Commander's code with the same result. The crackling pulsed loud and soft, but there was no sign that it was going to clear. Veryan looked worriedly at Randal.

"It's never done that before."

Randal fiddled with the equipment for a few minutes, turning and pressing anything that looked likely to improve reception. Nothing worked. Finally, he switched it off.

"Do you know what I think?" he asked. Veryan shook his head. "There's only one thing that would make it behave like this. If the central control station wasn't functioning. Where is the control for this region?"

"In Altir. Do you mean there's a fault at the station?"

Randal paused, wondering what to say. However much Veryan had changed, the change was still very recent and Randal did not want to frighten him.

Slowly, he replied, "There are usually back-up systems if faults develop. This sort of thing, well, it might mean that the station is completely out of action. Suppose that—"

"Suppose there's been another attack on Altir?"

In the end, Veryan had said it for him. Randal eyed him

uneasily, remembering how distraught he had been during the first attack. Veryan smiled faintly.

"Don't worry, Randal, I'm not going to panic. But what do you think we should do?"

"What do you want to do?"

Instead of answering right away, Veryan drifted across the room and sat in front of the computer where he usually worked, resting his head on one hand. He looked confused.

"Randal," he asked, "what would be the easiest way of finding out what really happened?"

"Take the flyer down to Carador," Randal replied promptly. "That's the nearest town. They may have had some news there."

Veryan was watching Randal, wide-eyed. "But the Commander said you're breaking the law if you take the flyer up."

Randal shrugged.

"This might be more important. Besides, there's some sort of loophole in the novice license regulations—'in an emergency or to save a life'—something like that."

Veryan nodded seriously. "Then perhaps we should do that Randal. Because the Governor has left me here now for four days without anyone in charge. And you know the way he fusses."

"Fusses" was not the word Randal would have chosen, but he let it pass.

"If there was an attack and he couldn't get through on the radio, then he would come out here to tell me and make sure I was safe." Veryan's features grew shadowed. "Unless he couldn't come. Unless he's injured—or dead."

Randal and Veryan left for Carador the next morning. They gave the housekeeper instructions to keep trying the radio and told her what to say to the Governor if he happened to arrive while they were out. Randal gained a lot of satisfaction from being able to pilot the flyer: not the feverish excitement of when he was doing wrong, just the knowledge that he was putting his skill to use.

The flight was short. Half an hour after they left the house they were approaching the outskirts of Carador. Randal looked out for a place to come down. Towns of any size all had a public landing field, but if he could avoid it he preferred not to answer questions about his novice license. Instead he carefully set the flyer down on a flat piece of ground about a mile outside the town, not far from the road.

He had already noticed a large number of other flyers in the air, more than would be usual for a small town like Carador. Some were taking off, some landing. Most of the arrivals seemed to be coming from the direction of Altir. Walking along the road into town, Randal began to feel uneasy.

He grew even more uneasy once they reached Carador. The streets were thronged with people moving here and there with no obvious purpose. There was a lot of pushing and jostling, and in a few places fighting had broken out. Most shops were closed. Inside one where the doors remained open, fruit and vegetables were spilled on the floor and people were looting. In a small square, flowers had been pulled up and trampled. Around one corner they saw a ground car tipped over on its side and burning. Veryan shrank closer to Randal.

"I don't like this," he said. "What's happening?"

"I don't know," Randal said. "Not an attack—there's no serious damage."

He was looking for a public radio point. At the first one he found, the equipment had been pulled away from the wall. The second was intact.

"Call the Governor," he said to Veryan.

Veryan keyed in the code. There was no screen, but from the earpiece came the familiar crackling sound. Randal was almost sure that his guess had been right. But while Veryan went on vainly trying to make the equipment work, he grabbed the arm of a young man who was hurrying past.

"What's going on?" he asked.

The man stared at him. "Haven't you heard? They smashed Altir—burnt it to the ground. And they'll be here next."

"But when did—" Randal started to ask. But the young man pulled away from him and hurried on.

Veryan replaced the earpiece.

"It's true, then."

"Yes. Let's get out of here."

They turned back the way they had come. Randal held on to Veryan's arm, afraid that they would be separated in the crowded streets. Crossing the square again they almost came to a halt, for it was packed with people listening to someone speaking from a balcony. The speech seemed to be all about war and defiance and the crowd yelled encouragement to the speaker. Randal did not pay much attention, but concentrated on pushing and elbowing his way along the edges, shielding Veryan as much as he could.

He thought they had broken free until three or four men lounging at the corner of the street leading away from the square stepped forward and barred their way.

"Where are you off to?" one of them asked.

He was tall, and broad without being fat. One look told Randal that he was dangerous.

"Excuse me, please," Randal said politely. "We have to go this way."

The man gathered his collar into one enormous hand. He pushed his face up close to Randal's.

"That's not what I asked."

"Oh, don't!" Veryan gasped.

He flung himself at the man, pulling at his arm in a futile attempt to free Randal. One of the others dragged him away, twisting his arms behind his back. Veryan cried out in pain, but went on fighting furiously. As he was trying to kick his captor a third man crashed a hand across his face. Then he began patting him all over, searching him. Randal felt almost relieved. They were petty thieves, then, and not something worse. The only thing Veryan was carrying of any interest was his father's Bible. It was slipped into an inside pocket. The man thumbed through it and then tossed it contemptuously into the road. He flung Veryan back against the wall where he crouched, gasping for breath.

Randal had more sense than to try struggling. He waited as the patting hands searched him, too, and endured without protest when the man took his watch and the little money he was carrying.

"Now get out," the first man said, pushing him away. "Get out and don't come back."

Still watching him warily, Randal went over to Veryan and helped him to his feet.

"Don't try anything stupid," he warned him.

As they moved away, Veryan stooped and caught up his Bible. Even that provoked a truculent growl from the man who had thrown it down, and Randal tugged at Veryan's arm to make him hurry. Glancing back, he saw that the men were lounging at the street corner again, watching them go. Their leader was grinning. Randal did not stop until they had turned the next corner and the men were out of sight.

Veryan was shaking, as much out of fury as fear. "I don't know how they dare!"

"They dare because there's no one left in Carador to stop them." Randal put an arm round Veryan's shoulders encouragingly. "Are you hurt?"

"No."

Veryan was still smoldering. Randal managed to smile at him.

"You did very well. But if we run into any more trouble, just keep quiet and let me handle it."

He was thankful that after that the crowds thinned out as they came to the edge of the town. Soon they were hurrying back along the road to the place where they had left the flyer.

"We'll go home and see if there's any word from the Governor," Randal decided. "And then we can—"

He broke off. They had come to the crest of a hill from where they should have been able to look down on the flyer. For a few seconds Randal wondered if they were on the wrong road. But he recognized the place and a cold hand twisted at his heart. The flyer was gone.

13

Randal, what's happened?" Veryan asked, bewildered.

"Someone must have stolen it." Randal was leaning on the stone wall that edged the road. He was gazing down into the field where they had left the flyer. "But I locked it! I know I did." His shoulders sagged. "Well, it's not difficult to break a lock, I suppose."

"What are we going to do?" Veryan asked.

He was giving Randal the familiar apprehensive look. Randal thought quickly.

"Get off this road to begin with," he said. "We don't know who might be around."

They climbed the wall into the field. Nearby, a stream trickled into a culvert under the road, and they crept into shelter at the mouth of the tunnel. There they would be unseen unless anyone came very close.

"We'd better walk back," Randal said. "We can probably make it before dark."

Veryan was frowning. "And then what? We can't get in touch with anyone if there's no radio. We can't stay up there for ever."

Randal thought over what he had said. It was true that if they went back to the house in the mountains they were no better off than they had been before. He was not sure that anyone was going to come looking for them, and only the Governor knew where they were. If he were, as Veryan feared, injured or dead. . . .

"The only other way would be to make for Altir," he said.

Veryan's frown disappeared. "All right," he agreed. "If you think that's best."

"Now just a minute!" Randal was astonished at Veryan's calm acceptance of their problem. He was not sure if it meant courage or sheer ignorance. "We've no food, no money, no transport. . . ."

"How long would it take to walk?" Veryan asked.

Randal paused, calculating. Judging distances was not his strong point, and he was used to traveling by shuttle or flyer or monorail, not on foot. He also had to allow for Veryan's strength, which might not hold out, for all his newfound spirit.

"Four, maybe five days," he hazarded. "We can't go without food for that long. I suppose we could go back into Carador and buy some," he added. "I can use my mother's credit."

"I don't want to go back there," Veryan said, "but if you think . . ."

Randal shook his head. "I doubt they would accept a credit code," he said. "It's like the radio. Everything's controlled from Altir, and if that's gone, well . . . Look, Veryan," he went on, "what we could do is go back to the house, get some food and sleeping bags and anything else we need and then—"

"Could you carry all that?" Veryan asked doubtfully. "I'm not sure I could. Besides, that would lose us nearly two days." He clasped his hands tightly together. "Randal, I'm frightened," he confessed. "I hate this. Now we know there's been another attack on Altir. The Governor could be dead. And my mother . . . I don't know whether she's on Centre or here on Barren or on a ship somewhere between. She might have gotten back to Altir before the attack and then . . ."

His voice quivered and he fell silent. He was obviously having a struggle to remain brave and optimistic. Randal could not help remembering his own blithe assumption that his father was indestructible.

"I'd like word of my father, too," he said slowly. "Veryan, are you really saying that you want to set out for Altir just as we are? Right now?"

Veryan brightened at once.

"Yes." Hesitantly, he added, "If it's the right thing to do—and I think it is—God will help us get there."

Randal made no comment. He was not sure he shared

Veryan's trust. If Veryan had said anything like that to him a few days ago he would probably have made some scathing comment. Now he was prepared to take Veryan's word for it. He heaved himself to his feet.

"I think we've both gone mad," he said. "But if that's what you want. . . ."

They scrambled through the culvert and out into the fields on the south side of the road.

As they walked, Randal tried to think ahead. There must be at least one main road from Carador to Altir. Using it would be much less tiring for Veryan than trekking across rough country. On the other hand, if refugees from Altir were making for Carador there might be trouble on the road.

Then Randal caught sight of a silver network curving across country in the distance. The monorail line. He had not taken that into account. He doubted that any trains would be running, but they could at least use the line to keep moving in the right direction. He pointed it out to Veryan and they struck across the fields toward it, though Randal did not want to get too close. It might be the target for another attack.

All that day they followed the monorail line. By the time the sun went down, Veryan was exhausted, stumbling along in silence with his head down. Even Randal was tired and hungrier than he had ever been in his life.

This is stupid, he thought. *We'll never do it. Veryan is finished already, but he won't admit it.*

As darkness gathered, he began looking for a sheltered place to pass the night. He could not help remembering the night they had spent in the forest with food to share and the certainty of being home safe the next day. Here there was scarcely a tree to break the flat expanse of fields, and no prospect of finding food that night or the next morning.

At last, when it was almost too dark to see, they came to a place where two narrow roads crossed each other. They were the first roads they had seen since they left Carador. Randal looked around cautiously. There was no sign of life or any buildings close enough to make out in the darkness. But someone must have been past recently, for in the angle of the crossroads a few bales of straw were carefully piled.

"We could stop here," Randal said. Veryan gave him a look out of shadowed eyes.

"I can go on if you want."

"No, it's too dark."

He shifted the bales around until he had built a small, three-sided shelter. Veryan sank to the ground where he huddled, shivering.

"I'm sorry, Randal," he said miserably. "I thought I would manage better than this."

Randal sat down beside him and put an arm round his shoulders. "You're not used to it, that's all." In spite of his own gloomy thoughts, he found himself saying, "We'll get on better tomorrow. As soon as it's light we'll look for somewhere we can find food."

"We can't pay for it."

"Well, maybe someone will let us work for it." He tried not to think of how long it would be before they were desperate enough to steal. "We'll manage something. Lie down and go to sleep."

Veryan murmured something and lay down. He was more content now that they had at least the beginnings of a plan for the next day. Randal took one more look around outside their shelter and settled down beside him. Veryan, already half asleep, curled up close to him for warmth. Randal was too hungry for sound sleep. He kept dozing and then waking up, his heart pounding, ready to fight or flee until he realized that the danger was only in his imagination. Then he would try to sleep again.

Toward morning he slept more soundly. A prodding in his ribs woke him. He stirred uncomfortably and muttered, "Veryan, stop it."

The prodding came again, harder and more painful. Randal opened his eyes. Beside him, Veryan was huddled, still deeply asleep. On the other side a booted foot was digging into him. Randal let his eyes travel upward until they met the barrel of a stun pistol, aimed directly at him. The man who held it was young, dark, and determined.

As Randal jerked upward, he said quietly, "No. Stay where you are. And tell me what you're doing on my land."

14

Faced with the stun pistol, Randal thought it might be better to do as he was told. He stayed where he was, half sitting up.

"We're not doing any harm," he said. "We just needed somewhere to sleep. We're trying to get to Altir."

"Get to Altir?" The man laughed. "Everybody else is trying to get away. I had half a dozen through here yesterday." He patted the pistol while making sure it stayed trained on Randal. "I saw them off."

Randal was still trying to think what to reply when Veryan, disturbed by his movement, roused and tried to sit up. His eyes widened as he saw the man with the pistol. "Randal, what?..."

Randal touched his arm reassuringly. "It's all right."

He was not at all sure that was true. Looking at Veryan who was white, disheveled, and still thoroughly confused by sleep and the sudden danger, he wondered how the man could possibly think they were a threat.

"Listen," he said to the man. "We need food, and—"

As if he had not spoken, the man stepped back and jerked the pistol. "Get up."

Warily, never taking his eyes off the man, Randal got to his feet and gave a hand to Veryan. Now that he was standing he could see a small truck—the kind a farmer might use—drawn up beside the road. Its engine purred softly.

"Now move." The man pointed down another of the four roads. "If you really want Altir, it's that way."

He jerked the pistol again in the direction he had shown them, a tight, controlled gesture. Randal had no doubt that he meant to use it.

"All right," he said. "We're going. Come on, Veryan."

He moved out of the shelter of the bales and toward the road. Veryan took a step or two, following him. Then he paused, swaying, with a hand to his head.

"Randal, I can't," he said. "I feel dizzy. I'm going to fall."

Randal darted back to his side and got an arm round him for support. Veryan sagged against him. Randal faced the man with the pistol. There was nothing to say.

For the first time the man looked uncertain.

"What's the matter with him?" he asked.

"We haven't eaten since yesterday morning," Randal said. "We've walked from Carador. He isn't strong. He can't go any further. Shoot us if you want to."

The man hesitated. Randal held his eyes without flinching. At last the man tucked the pistol away in his belt and gestured toward the truck.

"Get him in there."

Randal half carried Veryan across to the truck. A single seat stretched across the front of the driver's cab. With a push from Randal, Veryan managed to climb in and looked back at him apprehensively.

"Randal, I'm sorry."

"Don't be." Randal grinned at him. "I think you timed that pretty well."

Meanwhile, the farmer had started to load the bales of straw into the back of the truck. Wanting to show how willing he was, Randal helped him.

"Do you farm around here, sir?" he asked.

The man nodded with a flicker of surprise at the "sir."

"Fruit," he said curtly. "My neighbor over there . . ." he pointed, "he experiments with new strains of wheat. He lets me have the straw for packing." As he heaved the last bale on board and fastened the tailgate, he added, "My name's Emrys."

Randal introduced himself and Veryan. He wondered if Veryan's name might have meant something, but Emrys clearly did not connect him with the Governor of Altir. Or perhaps he just was not interested. He climbed into the driver's seat and

Randal scrambled up on the other side. Skillfully Emrys reversed the truck at the crossroads and began driving back the way he had come. The road was uneven. The truck bounced along cheerfully so that Randal had to concentrate on staying in his seat and supporting Veryan who had drifted into semi-consciousness. His head rested on Randal's shoulder.

Before long the road began to wind downward into a valley. At the bottom a river traced a wide loop where Randal could see about a dozen domes glistening in the sunlight like a cluster of soap bubbles. A squat, white house was built close beside them. Here Emrys drew up the truck, switched off the engine and slid out of the cab.

"Mira!" he called.

By the time Randal had helped Veryan down from the cab, a woman had appeared in the doorway. She looked surprised and a little nervous.

"My wife, Mira," Emrys introduced her, and explained, "I found these two by the crossroads. Reckon they wouldn't say no to some breakfast. Going to Altir, so they say."

He seemed to think no more explanations were necessary and got on with unloading his bales.

"Going to Altir?" Mira asked, standing back to let them into the house. "Nobody goes there now. Not since the attack. Haven't you heard?"

"We want to find our family," Randal explained, not wanting to go into a lot of complicated detail.

Mira clicked her tongue disapprovingly. She had already taken in Veryan's condition and moved to guide him along the passage.

"There are plenty of people leaving Altir," she went on. "At first we tried to help, but some of them are looking for trouble." She flung open a door and motioned them into the sunlit room beyond. "You two don't look dangerous," she added, smiling.

Deftly she eased Veryan into a cushioned chair by the window, looking out across a stretch of grass toward the domes. All the while he had been murmuring thanks and apologies for being a nuisance. Randal caught Mira's rather puzzled look before she turned away. He hid a smile. He was used to Veryan now, but he supposed that anyone else would be surprised to find such a fragile little aristocrat abandoned miles from anywhere and on the verge of collapse.

Mira left the room and came back a short while later with a tray. Her eyes danced amusement at Randal's eager look. She had brought hot, milky drinks, rolls and butter, and a bowl of fruit. Randal found that the fruit was delicious—better even than what had been served in the Governor's house.

"Emrys grew those," Mira explained, with unconcealed pride. "You can't buy some of the strains yet. Each of the domes has a different temperature and humidity so he can grow different things. We're planning to expand next year." Her expression grew troubled. "At least, we were. Now, after these attacks . . . well—" she straightened up determinedly. "We can only hope and pray."

As Randal listened, he began to realize that the attack on Altir was not just a passing thing—not a problem that could be cleared up quickly. Even when they reached the city, even if they found the Governor unharmed, the effects of the attack would go on affecting people's lives for years. It would affect his own life. Resolutely he pushed the thought away. He would worry about that later.

Veryan had eaten a little and then fallen asleep in the chair. Mira brought a blanket and tucked it around him while Randal loaded the empty dishes on to the tray.

"Is there anything I can do to help you?" he asked.

He rather regretted the question a little later when he found himself in front of a computer again, bringing up to date the records of crop yields from Mira's scribbled notes. Later still, everyone, including a revived Veryan, met for a meal in the farmhouse kitchen.

"Stay here tonight," Emrys invited, "and I'll take you on your way tomorrow."

Randal could hardly believe the offer and felt he had to protest. But Emrys explained.

"I've deliveries to make. Not as far as Altir—I doubt there's anyone there now who wants what I've got or can pay my prices. But I deliver to a few farms and villages in that direction. Help me load and unload and I'll drop you off as far as I go."

They set off in the truck the next morning as Emrys had promised with food packed for them by Mira. By midafternoon they had made their last delivery. Emrys drove a little further along the road.

"About a mile ahead," he said as he drew to a halt at last, "this road joins the main highway from Altir to Carador. If I were you, I'd keep well away. Go across country. You'll have to sleep out tonight, but you'll get to Altir tomorrow." He hesitated and added, "If you get there at all."

Slowly, he shook hands with Veryan and then with Randal. They got down from the cab and turned back to say good-bye.

"If things go wrong," Emrys said, "if you don't find the people you're looking for, you can come back to us." He interrupted their thanks, looking almost embarrassed. "We've got to help each other at a time like this."

Without saying any more, he put the truck into reverse, turned, and drove off in the direction of his home. Randal and Veryan called out to thank him again as they watched the truck disappear up the road. Then, once more, they set their faces toward Altir.

They reached the city on the evening of the following day. Although Veryan was growing tired again, they had not found the journey too hard. They were helped by Mira's provisions and the knowledge that they had not much farther to go. It was entering Altir that was most difficult of all.

Randal remembered the city as he had seen it on his first arrival. It had been spruce and shining and well-ordered. Now everything was changed. Swaths of destruction cut across the city: whole tracts of ground where nothing stood, where smoke still rose in sullen whorls from mounds of rubble. Within a few yards of the devastation, buildings were still standing, apparently undamaged. But many of them looked empty, as if their occupants had abandoned them. Unlike Carador, the streets were almost deserted.

CHAPTER 14

"What do you want to do?" Randal asked Veryan.

"Go home, I suppose," Veryan replied. "At least, to see what's left. If the Governor isn't there we could try the city offices, but they'll be closed at this time."

If they're still open at all, Randal thought. "All right," he said aloud. "Lead on."

From his previous visit, he knew that the park which surrounded the Governor's residence was close to the center of the city. As they drew nearer, he kept catching glimpses between buildings of trees and white walls. The residence was on a hill and it seemed almost unscathed. There was a defense screen, he remembered, which would have protected the house from the worst of the attack.

The approach to the main gate was across a square. The very edge of the attack had crumbled a building in one corner, but that was the only visible damage. The gate itself stood open and figures could be seen moving in and out of the small gatehouses on each side. Something about their appearance made Randal uneasy. At first he was not sure why until he realized they were not wearing the green uniform of the Governor's staff.

"Do you know them?" he asked Veryan.

Veryan shook his head. "I only ever saw the indoor servants." Nervously, he said, "Randal, I don't like this. Can we go somewhere and think it over first?"

Randal hesitated. It was almost dark. They saw the men at the gate only in the light coming from the gatehouses. Soon they would have to decide about shelter for the night. The thought of a bed in the Governor's house was very tempting, but he too did not like the look of the gate guards.

"Yes, we can . . . " he began, only to be interrupted by a shout from the gate.

Two of the guards were hurrying toward them. Randal's instinct was to turn and run, but he knew Veryan would be too exhausted to escape that way. They waited until the guards came up.

"Yes?" Randal said, trying hard to sound polite.

Close now, the guards were even more intimidating. They

were rough and unshaven. They wore dirty workmen's overalls with some kind of badge stitched clumsily to the sleeve.

"What're you doing?" the first guard asked. "Don't you know curfew's in five minutes?"

"I'm sorry," Randal said. "We've only just arrived. We didn't know about a curfew."

"Only just arrived?" the other guard asked, sneering. "What sort of a story is that? Nobody arrives here—not anymore. Where do you live?"

Randal flinched as Veryan, obviously shaken and too tired to think straight, decided to answer the question truthfully.

"In there," he replied, indicating the gates. "If you let us through, we'll be home in five minutes. I'm the Governor's son."

Randal had never seen anyone's expression change faster. From being defiant, half-enjoying the fun of baiting someone weaker, the guards had become alert, avid. One of them slid something from his belt—not a stun pistol this time, but a long, dangerous-looking knife. Veryan recoiled.

"The Governor's son," the guard said softly. "Well, isn't that useful? You're just the person we'd like to have a word with."

15

The two guards herded Randal and Veryan toward the gates where other guards clustered around them. Veryan was shrinking against Randal, bewildered and beginning to be frightened.

"Look what we've got here, lads," the first guard said. "The Governor's son!"

A murmur of voices, threatening but in some way approving, broke out around them. One of the men dragged Veryan forward so that he stood in the gateway where he could see the white walls of the house through gaps in the trees. The guard bent down and spoke close to Veryan's ear.

"Your father, he's in there," he said softly. "We'd like to have a chat with him, but he's got the defense screens up and he won't come out. Now, I reckon he'll come out fast enough when he finds out we've got you down here."

Veryan turned toward Randal, struggling in the man's grip. Randal did not know what to do. There were too many guards. They could not have fought their way out even if Veryan's strength had not been failing.

"Randal!" Veryan called out.

He was close to panic. Randal pushed his way through the men to his side, determined that whatever happened they were not going to be separated. He reached Veryan who clung to him, and for a moment they swayed together in the mass of guards surrounding them. Then a new voice broke in, clear and incisive.

"What's going on here?"

Falling back a pace or two from Randal and Veryan, the guards parted, allowing the new arrival to approach. Randal was gaping. He had already recognized the voice. It was Damaris.

She came to a halt beside Randal and gave him the friendly smile he had last seen on the shuttle.

"Hello, Randal," she said. "Having trouble?" To the guard, she repeated, "What's going on? What are you doing?"

To Randal's astonishment, the guard seemed to respect Damaris. He even touched his forehead in a clumsy salute.

"No more'n our duty, miss. This one here, he says he's the Governor's son."

Damaris looked Veryan up and down. Her brows rose.

"Really?" she said. "And you believe him? Have you ever seen the Governor's son looking like that?"

Randal caught on to her strategy. He was hard put to it not to grin. Veryan—hair tangled, filthy, exhausted after his travels, terrified by his present position—looked as little like the Governor's son as it was possible to imagine. Randal only hoped that the guards would not notice the expensive cut and fabric of the clothes that were now torn and stained.

The guard was looking embarrassed.

"Well, miss," he was saying, "that's what he told us. He don't look crazy."

"They don't," Damaris said crisply. "Well, they're not crazed, poor things. They've just been through more than they can cope with. I had one down at the center the other day. Absolutely convinced he was the fleet admiral. Sounded very sensible, too. But he changed his mind after a good meal and a night's rest. I'll take charge of this one if you like."

Randal realized that the guards were moving away, their mood changing. Beyond all hope, Damaris had convinced them.

"I know his friend," she told the guards. "We'll look after him. Randal, will you bring him down to the center?"

Randal was only too glad to agree and gasp out his thanks. Veryan looked completely bewildered. Randal hoped that he would keep quiet until they were well away.

"We'll go then," Damaris said. "I'm out after curfew, I'm afraid. But I've got a pass. I've been delivering medicine. I'll get these two under cover. Don't worry."

With a friendly nod to the guards, she turned away. Randal urged Veryan to follow her and no one tried to stop them. Even so, Randal felt a prickling at his back as the guards watched them go. He could not be really at ease until they had left the square and turned into a quiet street.

"Damaris, that was brilliant!" he exclaimed. "You really made them believe you! I don't know how—"

Damaris came to a sudden halt.

"What do you mean, I made them believe me? Why shouldn't they believe me?" Her gaze narrowed as Randal, beginning to understand, stifled laughter. "Are you saying that he really is? . . ."

Her gaze swiveled to Veryan.

"I'm so sorry," Veryan said, summoning politeness even though he was leaning on Randal's arm to stay on his feet. "I suppose I was stupid to tell them so, but I'm really not out of my mind. The Governor is my stepfather."

Damaris was frowning.

"So I told those men a pack of lies? Honestly, Randal, you could have . . ." Her irritation dissolved in a gurgle of laughter. "No, I don't suppose you could." She shrugged, dismissively. "You'd better come to the center," she said. "I've a pass to be out after curfew, but even so, there could be trouble if we're caught hanging around."

She moved off down the street again, slowly, so that Randal, helping Veryan, could keep pace with her.

"So what's going on?" she asked. "Randal, you told me you were leaving Altir with your cousin, and now—"

"Veryan is my cousin. I'm sorry, I haven't introduced you. Veryan, this is Damaris."

"How do you do?" Veryan murmured. "Randal told me about you. Thank you for helping us."

Damaris looked slightly startled and then her smile returned.

"I'm sorry. I hadn't realized the sort of company I'm keeping," she said. "But you still haven't explained, Randal, what you're doing back in Altir."

While they made their way to the medical center Randal

told Damaris what had happened since they last spoke. He skipped over the details of his own campaign to be sent back, concentrating instead on Veryan's anxiety about the Governor and the details of their journey from Carador. The recital lasted until they reached the center.

"I can't believe you'd be so stupid," Damaris said frankly. "You could easily have gotten yourselves killed."

She tapped in a code on the panel of a side door at the center and it slid back to admit them.

"Come in," she invited, and added to Veryan, "We'd better get you to bed."

"I'm not ill," Veryan said determinedly. "Just tired. And I'd rather talk if you have the time. I need to know what's happened in Altir."

"All right," Damaris agreed. "But I've a few things to do first. Would you like a shower? You look as if you need it, if you don't mind my saying so. And by the time you've both finished I should be free."

She led them along a passage and up a flight of stairs to a small room containing nothing but two beds and lockers. There was a shower room next door. The lockers held towels and robes.

"All the comforts of home," Damaris pointed out and whisked away.

Randal could scarcely wait to peel off his filthy clothes and get into the shower. But since there was a curtly worded notice beside the shower about not wasting water, he spent the least time there that he could, while still being reasonably clean.

When Veryan had finished, he got into bed. Randal propped up a few pillows for him, since Veryan insisted that he did not mean to go to sleep. He was drowsing, however, by the time Damaris returned.

She had brought mugs of soup, bread, and cheese with her for all three of them.

"I'll have my supper with you," she said, "and then we can talk. Tell me what you need to know."

Randal looked at her over the top of his mug. "Everything," he said.

Damaris lifted her brows slightly but made no other comment. She settled herself comfortably on the end of Veryan's bed.

"You realize there was a second attack," she began. "Oh, days ago, now. I'm losing count. The city offices were destroyed and there was no city government left. The Governor was nowhere to be seen." She gave Veryan a brief, apologetic glance. "Since everybody was blaming him and out for his blood, I suppose it's understandable. They say he's in his house, but he won't come out. And no one else can get in through the defense screen, so they've circled the wall with guards so he can't slip away secretly."

Now Randal understood better what the guards had been saying.

"But if there's no government," he said, "who put the guards there? Whose are they?"

"I didn't say there was no government," Damaris pointed out. "We've got a new one, for what it's worth. There's a man calling himself Warden, and he's giving the orders now. He's got a whole horde of people, like those guards you met, making sure his orders are obeyed." Her voice held a withering disapproval. "One thing he did was impose a curfew. But that's not the worst. . . ."

"Well?" Randal asked, when she hesitated.

"I can't understand it," Damaris said. "He says that all machines and books are evil. It's a crime now to operate machinery, or to possess a book. The Warden's men have the authority to break into people's houses, smashing and burning—"

"But why?" Veryan asked.

He was curled up against his pillows, hands clasped round his mug, his eyes enormous. He followed everything Damaris was telling them with painful concentration.

"He says it's because we used the books and the machines to fight the war. And if they're all destroyed the war will have to end."

"I can understand that," Veryan said.

"Yes, but he and his men don't see any difference between a piece of machinery like a gun that's used for killing, and something peaceful, like the radio. You might have noticed that the radio's out. The station wasn't damaged in the attack. It was the Warden's men. The same with books. They burned them all. Yesterday they set fire to the central library. They beat up anybody they find carrying something forbidden. We've had them here. We're not looking after war casualties, you know, or not many, just people who've met the Warden's mobs."

She was flushed with anger, her hands clenched tightly together.

"But you must be using machinery here," Randal said.

"Yes, for the time being." Damaris took a deep breath, consciously trying to stay calm. "Even the Warden's men seem to realize that they need medical services. So far they've left us alone. There's no power, so we're running on emergency power packs and they won't last for ever. We're expecting the water to go off any day now." Her anger suddenly replaced by weariness, she leaned back against the wall, pushing back a stray strand of hair. "I don't know how long we can keep going. I just pray and take it a day at a time."

"You're not by yourself are you?" Randal asked.

Damaris grinned tiredly.

"Do I sound as if I've got the whole world on my shoulders? No, there's Doctor Sorel. She's the head of the center. And there's her deputy, Doctor Mayne as well as some more helpers like me. But we've had to send people out to other places like Carador." She drained her mug and reached out to put it on top of the locker. "That's enough about me. Now tell me what you want to do."

Randal had no reply. For days now he had thought no further than the immediate need for food and shelter. It was Veryan who replied, with the obstinate look that was becoming familiar.

"I don't know. I suppose we'll have to leave Altir in the end. But I'm not going until I find out what's happened to the Governor."

16

The next morning Damaris brought fresh clothes for Randal and Veryan. She and Randal had talked far into the previous night after Veryan had finally succumbed to sleep. There seemed nothing to do except stay at the center and hope that somehow there would be a way to make contact with the Governor.

"At least we can help," Randal said. He summoned a grin. "I said I would join your project!"

He was less enthusiastic the next day when he found himself cleaning floors with a mop and a bucket of water. He had never seen anything so primitive in his life. Damaris was unsympathetic.

"We keep the power for essentials," she said.

Randal was still mopping away busily when he became conscious of a sound—a sound that had been there for some time before he asked himself what it was. It was faint because it was distant, but when he stopped work to listen he could discern an irregular pounding noise, shouts, and the trampling of feet. He left his mop propped against the wall and went out into the passage.

Following the sound, he came to a flight of stairs which led into the main entrance hall of the center. Damaris was already there with Veryan and others of the staff. The pounding was louder now, coming from outside of the main door, and one voice was raised above all the others.

"Open in the Warden's name!"

Randal crossed the hall to stand beside Damaris.

"What's going on?" Damaris looked grim.

"Trouble."

The order from outside was repeated and the door shook

under the pounding, though the lock held. In the hall, the staff looked at each other uncertainly. No one moved to open it or replied to the voice.

Randal was wondering how long the door would hold when a brisk footstep sounded behind him. Looking around, he saw a tall, gray-haired woman in a doctor's white overall.

She came to a halt in the center of the hall, took in the situation with a single glance, and ordered crisply, "Open the door."

The young man who was standing nearest to the door release button protested.

"But Doctor Sorel—"

"Open it."

With a helpless look at his nearest companion, the young man obeyed. The door slid back. The noise died. In the doorway stood three men dressed like the guards Randal had seen at the Governor's residence the night before. He could tell by the badges stitched to their sleeves. Behind them, pushing and swaying on the steps of the center and as far beyond as Randal could see, was a crowd of people. A hostile muttering still rose from them. Randal felt Veryan's hand on his arm, and it occurred to him for the first time to be afraid.

Doctor Sorel stood facing the three men.

"Yes?" she inquired. "How may I help you?"

The man in the middle stepped forward. "Doctor Sorel?"

"Yes."

The man pulled out a paper from the pocket of his overalls. "I've a warrant for your arrest, Doctor. And for Doctor Mayne. He is here?"

"Doctor Mayne," Doctor Sorel said evenly, "is at present in the middle of an operation. He cannot be disturbed."

In the doorway the crowd swayed forward threateningly. The Warden's officer cast an uncertain look over his shoulder.

Blustering, he said, "You can't ignore the Warden's warrant."

"May I ask what we are charged with?" Doctor Sorel interrupted, still icily calm.

That question was one to which the man knew the answer.

CHAPTER 16

Recovering some of his authority, he began to recite.

"Operating machinery, Doctor, in violation of the Warden's Fourth Edict. Possession of books, papers, and computer disks in violation of the Fifth Edict."

Doctor Sorel gave a thin smile.

"Is that all?" she asked. "No theft? Murder? Treason?"

"It's treason all right!" somebody shouted from the crowd. A roar of agreement rose from their throats.

"Yes, Doctor," the officer said. "It's treason now to keep anything that could be used for the war."

"Since the Warden and his men are so passionately opposed to violence," Doctor Sorel said.

Her eyes raked across the mob outside. She stepped neatly around the officer and stood at the top of the steps, ignoring his attempt to grab her arm. When she spoke, her voice was raised, not to a shout, but with the clarity she might have used in a lecture theater. The crowd listened.

"All the machinery we have here," she said, "is for the saving of life. Any one of you may come here for help if you need it. If you smash our machinery today, you may need our help tomorrow—you, or your wives and children. Think about that before you go any further."

From where he was standing, Randal could not see clearly. But he had the impression that at least some of the crowd were dispersing. Certainly they were much quieter. Doctor Sorel stood looking down at them for a moment longer and then turned back to the officer.

"If this is treason," she said, "I am ready to answer the charge."

Before the officer could pull himself together, another man appeared from the back of the hall. He was an older man, plump and bald with a harassed expression.

"Doctor Sorel!" he exclaimed. "What's all—"

"Is the operation finished?" Doctor Sorel asked.

"Yes, quite routine," the man, whom Randal took to be Doctor Mayne, replied. "The orderly is putting him to bed. But what . . ."

"We appear to be under arrest," Doctor Sorel told him.

"Under arrest? Never heard such nonsense in my life!" Doctor Mayne turned to the officer and prodded him in the chest. "Now listen to me, young man, and . . ."

Doctor Sorel interrupted him.

"I think we should go and answer the charges. There will be no peace here until we do." Doctor Mayne looked as if he were going to protest and then shrugged, half smiling.

"Have it your way, my dear. You always do."

Under the escort of the officers, the two doctors moved toward the door. The rest of the staff were watching, stunned, except for the young man who had opened the door. He stepped forward and began to speak.

"You can't—"

Doctor Sorel laid a hand on his arm.

"It's for the best. We'll go and talk some sense into these people. I don't suppose we'll be away long."

Head held high, she led the way down the steps and the crowd parted to let her through. Damaris began pushing her way through the assembled staff toward the door.

"I don't think she knows what she's talking about!" she said. "She can't talk sense to the Warden. People like that don't listen. I'm going with her."

"What can you do?" Randal asked.

"I don't know. Bring back word of what happens, if nothing else. Because I don't think they'll be coming home in a hurry."

"I'll go with you," Randal said.

Outside, the doctors and their escort were lost in the crowd, sweeping back down the steps and along the street. Damaris and Randal tagged on to the edge. A voice spoke at Randal's elbow.

"Where are they taking them?"

Momentarily Randal had forgotten Veryan.

"You shouldn't be here," he said. "It might be dangerous." Veryan just gave him his stubborn look. Randal knew there was no point in arguing with that. Meanwhile Damaris was answering the question.

"The Warden's headquarters is in the old Law Courts," she

said. "Very suitable, don't you think? That's where we're going. They'll be tried right away."

The pace of the crowd had quickened. More people joined them so that Randal, Damaris, and Veryan were wedged in the middle, carried along whether they wanted to go or not. They were holding on to each other so as not to be separated. They turned a corner. Randal saw ahead of him a large, white building with a pillared porch and steps leading up to its doors. The people at the front of the crowd were already pouring up the steps.

Inside the crowd was denser still. It was difficult to move, but Damaris pushed her way through and Randal followed, trying to shield Veryan from being carried off his feet. Eventually they came to a circular hall. Rank after rank of benches sloped down to a platform in the center. All the seats were crammed with people. They were sitting on the steps in the aisles and thronging the passage at the back of the benches. Randal thought that for such a large crowd they were unnaturally quiet. Then he fought his way forward a little and realized that the trial of Doctor Sorel and Doctor Mayne had already begun.

Looking down at the platform he could make out the two doctors, very small at this distance, standing before three others who were seated side by side. Doctor Sorel was speaking. Randal strained to hear what she was saying, but there was no loudspeaker system in operation. He could only catch a few words. He thought that she was repeating in more detail what she had said on the steps of the medical center. Randal could not make out clearly the features of the three listeners or guess how they were responding.

"Is that the Warden?" he said into Damaris's ear.

"Yes, the one in the middle. Shh."

When Doctor Sorel had finished there was a pause in which the three listeners—judges, Randal said silently to himself— conferred together. A murmur of conversation, a buzz like a hive of gigantic bees, rose from the watching crowd. Randal turned to speak to Damaris and saw her eyes fixed. Her lips moved silently—in prayer, he realized. Half ashamed of himself, still not sure if there was any point in it, he added his own words, equally silent, "God, if there is anything You can do, then do it now. Please."

He did not know what sort of response he was expecting. What happened was that the Warden rose to his feet, raised his arms for silence, and began to speak. He was a tall, dark man, and he wore the same sort of uniform as his followers. He had raised his voice so that even those at the back of the hall, like Randal, could hear.

"This court passes sentence on Doctor Sorel and Doctor Mayne, charged with offenses under the Fourth and Fifth Edicts. The verdict of this court is that they are guilty as charged."

Randal felt Damaris dig her fingers painfully into his arm. A babble began in the crowd which the Warden silenced with a gesture.

"The sentence of this court is that they should both be assigned to work in the labor gangs for the duration of this emergency. Their evil books and machinery are to be destroyed. This trial is over."

Randal caught a glimpse of Doctor Sorel beginning to protest and being dragged off the platform by a group of the Warden's guards. The Warden and his fellow judges moved away. Then Damaris was tugging him toward the door.

"Come on!" she urged. "We've got to get back to the center. We've got to warn them!"

Because they had come in near the back of the crowd, it was not difficult for Randal, Damaris, and Veryan to thrust their way out into the street again. Behind them, the leaders of the mob were streaming down the steps of the Law Courts. Randal felt as if he were being hunted.

"We've got to hurry!" Damaris cried out. "If we're split up, meet back at the center!"

"Yes!"

Damaris drew ahead almost at once. Randal felt that he had to stay with Veryan who was tiring now. He was gasping for breath and finding it hard to keep up.

"You go on," he said. "I'll be all right."

"No point," Randal replied. He had taken Veryan's arm and was hurrying him on as best he could. "Damaris will warn them."

He did not like to ask himself what she or the rest of the staff at the center could do against the mob that was bearing down on them now. Somewhere among them would be the Warden's guards. But they would hardly be needed to carry out the sentence. The crowd, the people of Altir, maddened by fear of the war and convinced they had to destroy the "evil" around them, would do it for them.

They had not gone much farther when the first of the horde overtook them, washing around them like a flood tide. They were pushed from side to side. Veryan stumbled and would have fallen except for Randal's support. Raucous shouting was all around them. They could do no more than stay on their feet and let the crowd carry them along.

The advancing mob filled the whole of the street. Those

passing by who were trying to move in the opposite direction were thrust aside or caught up in the main flow of people and forced along with them. Here and there at the edges fights were breaking out. If this was the answer to prayer, then what was the point in praying? Randal wondered.

They swept around the corner that brought the medical center into sight. Randal was trying to peer over the heads of the crowd. As he was trying to see what was happening in front of him, he heard a sharp cry from Veryan. Afraid he was hurt, Randal turned to him. But at the same instant Veryan tore away from him and darted through a gap in the heaving mass of people. Randal lost sight of him.

"Veryan!" he shouted.

There was no reply. Randal flung himself in the same direction, fighting to get through. But he was carried along past the place where he had lost Veryan. After a minute or two he was struggling to move against the flow of the crowd. He slipped and would have gone down if he had not grabbed at somebody who shook him off, but not before he had regained his feet.

"Veryan!" he cried out helplessly.

There was still no response. Inexorably, for all his efforts, Randal was carried on down the street.

By the time he reached the medical center, the main doors were open and the crowds were thrusting their way in. Randal went with them, managing to force his way to the edge and fetching up against the wall of the entrance hall. He stood there, panting.

Beyond him he could hear shouting and the crash of shattering machinery. From one doorway black smoke billowed out. As he watched, Damaris appeared, head down, arms clasped around a pile of books. She fled for the stairs. A half dozen men followed her. Randal started to follow, too, shouting her name as he flung himself upward. Then someone grabbed him from behind. His foot slipped and this time there was nothing to hold on to, nothing as he fell backward, clutching at emptiness. He went down into exploding darkness.

Randal opened his eyes on an expanse of white which he identified in a moment as a pillow. Almost at once he realized that he was lying on his own bed in his room at the center. He tried to sit up.

"Keep still," said Damaris's voice.

He obeyed and felt fingers gently touching the back of his head. It occurred to him that he had a pounding headache. The fingers stopped whatever they were doing and Damaris's voice spoke again.

"Now try to sit up."

Randal tried. He found it was more difficult than expected, but finally he managed it and leaned back against the wall for support.

"Going to be sick?" Damaris asked him. Randal considered it.

"I don't think so."

"Good."

She began to clear away the bowl of water and the dressings she had used to bandage his head. When he looked at her closely, Randal realized he had never seen her like this. He had never seen her at all except when she was brave and cheerful and competent. Now she was filthy: the collar of her tunic torn, and her face streaked with dust. There were marks on her face that told him she had been crying and had not had time to wash afterwards.

"Are you all right?" he asked.

"Oh, yes." She tried to smile; it was not her best effort. "Not a scratch on me. I scratched a few of them, though."

"Is it bad?" Randal asked, afraid of what the reply would be.

"If you're fit to walk," she said, "you can come and see."

Randal followed her downstairs. The first room she showed him was the one where the smoke had been pouring out. In the middle of the floor was a mound of black ash. It was just possible to see that books and papers had been burned there. The floor was filled with water.

"The sprinkler system cut in," Damaris explained. "That's built in, so it was a bit harder to smash. They got it in the end, though."

The next room had been used for storing medicines. The cabinets had been smashed and the floor was strewn with crushed packets, spilled powder and liquid, and broken glass. One of the orderlies was picking his way cautiously through it, trying to see what could be salvaged. He looked up when he realized Randal and Damaris were there.

"They didn't have to do this," he said bitterly. "This wasn't books or machinery. This doesn't come under their precious Edicts. They even burned the stock list."

Damaris tugged at Randal's arm and led him into the operating theater. The table itself was lying on its side. Around it was a scatter of machinery, casings split open. Components were spilling out. Randal did not know what most of them were used for, but he doubted that they would be much use for anything now.

"Have you seen enough?" Damaris asked. Randal nodded, feeling sick.

"They've even smashed the kitchen," she said. "I don't know how we're going to cook or even boil water. Perhaps over an open fire if there is anywhere to put one."

She led Randal out into the main hall again.

"I'm supposed to be patching up the injured," she said. "We've set up our headquarters in the staff lounge—down there." She pointed. "Go and ask them to find you a job to do."

She had begun to move off when Randal stopped her.

"Damaris," he asked, "where's Veryan?"

Damaris hesitated, staring at him. "I don't know. He was with you."

Randal's sick feeling became a hollow in the pit of his stomach. "He dashed off into the crowd. I tried to find him, but I couldn't. I thought he would have come back here. Damaris, are you sure? . . ."

"He's not here," she said.

Thoroughly frightened, Randal crossed the hall and looked out of the main door. The street was empty now except for one or two people hurrying furtively past, and one or two motionless bodies lying where they had fallen. None of them was Veryan.

CHAPTER 17

"I'll have to go and look for him," Randal said. "If he comes back, make him stay here."

"Nobody makes Veryan do anything," Damaris said pointedly, as she went back to her work.

If he had not been so worried, Randal would have grinned. Damaris had never met Veryan before the day on the mountain. She was not aware of how much he had changed. But now Randal almost wished the change had never happened. The timid little creature Veryan had been would never have gone plunging into danger like that.

Randal hurried down the steps into the street. He had lost Veryan near the corner, but the crowd should have carried him on after that. He walked rapidly down the street, looking from side to side. In the midst of his quest he found that he was praying again, "Don't let the stupid little idiot be badly hurt," as if he had any confidence left after the result of his earlier prayer.

He had reached the corner when he heard Veryan's voice, speaking quietly behind him.

"Randal . . . oh, Randal!"

Randal whirled. Veryan was curled up in the entrance porch of a boarded-up shop, a sheltered place that would have been out of the main press of the crowd. Another man was huddled beside him, unmoving with his head in Veryan's lap. Veryan had an arm protectively around his shoulders. Randal stepped forward.

"And just what do you think you've been doing?" he asked dangerously.

"I saw him in the crowd," Veryan explained. His face looked drawn, and his hair disheveled. His voice was shaking for all his efforts to keep it steady. "Someone pushed him and he fell. I couldn't leave him, could I?"

Still not sure he understood, Randal bent over by Veryan's side. He saw the man's face clearly for the first time. It was haggard, unshaven, and dabbled with blood that trickled from a cut on the forehead. But there was no mistaking the scar. The man was Commander Farre.

Randal reached for the Commander's wrist, fumbled for his pulse and found it. He was breathing but his eyes were closed.

"I think he hit his head when he fell," Veryan said. "I don't know how serious it is. He was conscious at first and I tried to help him along to the center, but he couldn't manage it. I think his leg is hurt again. I couldn't carry him by myself, so I thought we'd better wait here." His eyes met Randal's trustfully. "I knew you would come, Randal."

Randal, who had been thinking of various scathing things that he might say, found himself left speechless. He watched Veryan, who was bending over the Commander, repeating his name and trying to make him respond. After a few seconds his eyes fluttered open and he raised one arm as if he were trying to ward off a blow.

"Oh, don't!" Veryan pleaded. "It's all right. It's only me—Veryan."

The Commander focused his eyes on him with difficulty.

"Veryan?" The once incisive speech was slurred. "It can't be. You shouldn't be here."

"We came back, sir," Randal said. Veryan's distress at the Commander's condition was making him almost unable to speak. "Can you get up? We'll take you to the medical center and have that cut seen to."

The Commander looked at him and shook his head vaguely. Randal was not sure if he were replying to the question, failing to recognize him, or just refusing to accept what he saw. After a moment he raised a shaking hand to his head. The fingers came away smeared with blood. He stared at it, uncomprehending.

Randal exchanged a glance with Veryan. Clearly the cut on the head was not the only thing wrong with the Commander. He put an arm around him to help him to his feet. But when the Commander tried to put his weight on his right leg, it gave way and he lurched to his knees.

"I'm sorry," he muttered. "This leg has never been much use. Not since . . ."

His voice died away into an almost inaudible murmur. Randal moved to support him on that side, and at the second try he managed to stand. They moved off slowly. Randal was alert for any sign of more trouble erupting on the street. Their progress was very slow and they would have been hard put to defend themselves.

They reached the medical center at last. In the entrance hall, Veryan paused, gazing around at the destruction he could see through the open doors.

"They really destroyed it all?" he whispered.

"Just about," Randal replied.

Since there was no one around to ask, they took the Commander to their own room and let him lie on Veryan's bed where he promptly gave up the fight to stay conscious.

"Randal, he's ill," Veryan said, looking down at the still figure. "What are we going to do?"

"Find someone to dress that cut," Randal replied.

He went in search of help. By the time he returned with an orderly, Veryan had brought water and was washing the blood from the Commander's face and hands. The cut had almost stopped bleeding.

"He'll do," the orderly said, as he deftly placed a dressing on it. "If he's fit to move, he'll have to leave as soon as he wakes up." He interrupted Veryan's protest. "We'll do the best we can, but we just can't be housing every vagrant who comes in off the streets. Not anymore."

He collected up his equipment and left.

"Vagrant!" Veryan said indignantly. "He's not . . ."

He broke off as the Commander's eyes opened once again. Swiftly he crouched beside the bed and took his hand.

"Commander? Do you feel better, sir?"

The Commander half smiled. "Veryan? I thought I'd dreamed that bit. Here in Altir . . . and Randal with you?"

"Here, sir," Randal said, sitting down on the bed where the Commander could see him. "We heard about the attack, so we thought we ought to come. Veryan is worried about the Governor. Do you know anything about him, sir?"

"He's too tired to answer questions," Veryan said protectively.

The Commander waved him away with a little of his old authority.

"No—no, I can talk. But there's not much I can tell you. I haven't seen him—not since he brought me back from the mountains. They say he's at the residence. . . ."

His voice faded. Clearly he was feeling more tired or ill than he was prepared to admit.

"That's what we heard," Randal said, discouraged. They were no closer to solving their problem. "And Veryan won't leave or do anything until he knows for certain that the Governor is all right."

The Commander's smile returned. "Well done," he murmured. "Climbing another mountain. . . ."

Veryan flushed and moved away to fetch a glass of water for the Commander. He had to support him and hold the glass for him while he drank.

Randal could not resist asking, "What happened to you, sir?"

The look the Commander gave him was helpless and almost apologetic.

"The building I lived in was destroyed in the attack. I wasn't in it at the time, but I lost everything except the clothes I was wearing. I'd nowhere else to go. I tried to find work, but there isn't much available in Altir just now unless you want to join the Warden's thugs. That I won't do. Besides, I believe the Warden has a preference for the able-bodied. . . ."

An expression of bitterness was settling in his eyes and around his mouth. Veryan caught at his hand again.

"So you've been wandering around Altir ever since the attack? Oh—" His voice almost broke, but he swallowed and went on, "It's over now, sir. We need you to help us. You'll be able to tell us how we can talk to the Governor."

The Commander started to speak and then broke off again at the sound of hurried footsteps. Damaris appeared at the door.

"Oh, you found him," she said, with a glance at Veryan. "You might have told me. Who is this?"

The look she gave the Commander suggested that he might be one more problem than she was prepared to deal with.

"Commander Farre," Randal replied. "He used to be our tutor."

"I found him in the street," Veryan said. "He's hurt."

Damaris's expression became one of active dislike.

"You're not one of the people who's responsible for this, are you?" she asked. "Because—"

"No!" Veryan interrupted hotly. "The Commander wouldn't have anything to do with it! He was . . ."

"Going the wrong way at the wrong time," the Commander interrupted wearily. "And if it hadn't been for Veryan . . ." He looked up at Veryan and reached a hand to him, smiling faintly. "Thank you."

Veryan flushed, embarrassed. He sat clinging to the Commander's hand.

"I don't even know what it was all about," the Commander said.

"The Warden's mob just smashed up the center," Damaris said. She was still angry, though not any longer with him. "Our doctors have been sentenced for violation of the Fourth and Fifth Edicts. Sentenced to labor gangs. . . ."

"Labor gangs?" Veryan echoed. "What's that?"

It was the Commander who replied. "Mostly repairing or clearing damaged buildings. Hefting stone and metal girders, by hand, of course, no machinery. I tried it for half a day, but my leg wouldn't hold up."

"Labor gangs!" Damaris repeated. "When they're trained, skilled people, and Altir needs them."

"What are you going to do now?" Randal asked.

Damaris shrugged. "The best we can. We've no fully trained

doctors anymore, but there are some quite competent people—except that all the machinery is smashed. There's a limit to what a person can do."

The Commander raised his head, looking a little more alert.

"Machinery? What kind of machinery?"

"Oh . . . monitoring equipment. Diagnostic aids. Surgical tools. All kinds of things. But they're lying around in pieces now. I suppose they might be repaired but no one here knows how."

"Well, I'm not sure," the Commander said diffidently, "but I rather think I might."

Damaris stared at him. Randal could see her anger and anxiety beginning to dissolve and her natural optimism reasserting itself.

"You're not a fleet medic are you?" she asked.

"I'm not a fleet anything," returned the Commander dryly. "But my specialist training was in electronics—mostly for communications systems, but the principle is roughly the same. If you'll show me. . . ."

He started to get up from the bed, swayed and sank back again.

"He's ill!" Veryan protested. "He can't do it, or not right away. He needs a rest and something to eat. I don't suppose you've had a proper meal since the attack?" he scolded.

"I can manage," the Commander said. "Though I wouldn't say no to the food."

"Randal, why don't you go and raid the kitchen?" Veryan suggested. "You're good at that."

Randal looked for a suitable object to throw at him, but failed to find anything, so he went.

By the time he had assembled a tray for himself, Damaris, and Veryan as well as the Commander, the others had moved downstairs to the operating theater. Someone had set the table upright again and the Commander was using it as a workbench. Damaris was prospecting among the wreckage.

"Start with the least damaged," the Commander was saying. "Or the most urgent."

"And hope they're the same. . . ." Damaris murmured. "Randal, mind where you're putting your feet."

CHAPTER 18

Randal navigated carefully across the room to the table and set down his tray.

"This was the best I could find," he said. "Cold, I'm afraid."

Damaris' glance swept over the tray with its odds and ends of bread, cheese, biscuits, and dried fruit.

"Better than nothing," she said. "And where the next meal is coming from, I don't know." Briefly she looked anxious and then shrugged. "Someone else will have to cope with that. Commander, if you haven't been eating regularly, don't overdo it now."

Randal would never have dared use that autocratic tone, but the Commander simply murmured, "No, of course not," and continued poking around among the components laid out on the table.

"Have you tools for this job?" he asked.

"Tools!" Damaris was briefly at a loss. "I'll find out," she said. "Wait a minute."

She whisked out of the room. While she was away, Veryan began to serve the food and Randal poured drinks from a container of fruit juice. By the time they had finished, Damaris was back. She was followed by an orderly carrying a box which he set down on the table in front of the Commander.

"This is what we have, sir," he said. "Will they do?" The Commander flipped open the lid of the box and nodded approvingly.

"Splendid."

The orderly started to leave and then at the door turned back.

"Have you heard the latest news?" he asked.

"No. What now?" Damaris said.

"The Warden has just issued another of his Edicts. He's sentenced the Governor to death."

19

Veryan took a sudden step forward. He had gone very white.

"Sentenced him?" he echoed. "Is he a prisoner? Has there been a trial?"

"No," the orderly said. His tone was casual. He had no idea who Veryan was or why the thought of the Governor's death should affect him. "As far as anyone knows, the Governor is still in the residence hiding behind his defense screen. I don't know why the Warden bothered to issue his Edict. I suppose it makes him feel good."

He shrugged and left. Veryan took a pace after him and then turned back to Randal and the others. He was twisting his hands together nervously.

"I've got to do something!" he said. "Somehow I've got to get him out of there."

"It strikes me that he's safer where he is," Damaris said.

"But he can't stay there forever! And things here are getting worse. I have to get him out of Altir."

"But you can't reach him," objected Randal. "You can't get through the guards or the defense screen. You can't even call him on the radio."

Randal could not help feeling that the Governor had only himself to blame for his problems. Instead of hiding away in the residence, he should have been out in the city trying to help his people. If he had done that, the Warden might never have come to power. More than anything, Randal did not want Veryan rushing into danger again.

"I know the code to switch the screen off," Veryan said. "But I haven't got a decoder."

CHAPTER 19

"I could make you one . . ." the Commander offered, ". . . if I had the components."

"There's a whole roomful of components," Damaris said, spreading her arms wide. "But that won't get you past the Warden's guards."

"No. . . ."

Veryan lapsed into thoughtfulness.

Randal gave him an uneasy look. "You shouldn't encourage him, sir," he said to the Commander.

The Commander smiled. "He doesn't need encouraging," he said. "Not anymore."

Remembering the food, Randal distributed plates and they ate in silence. Randal was trying not to think about the problems that faced them. He could not see how the center could keep running from day to day. The state of the city as a whole was too big for him to think about. He knew that Damaris and Veryan and perhaps even the Commander would do the job that was nearest and leave the rest to God. Randal wished he could feel the same.

When the meal was over, the Commander laid out his tools and began work on a heart monitor which had only minor damage.

"So tiny!" Damaris marveled.

"So far there's nothing wrong with my eyesight," the Commander retorted. Damaris grinned at him.

"Listen, Commander—" She broke off. "I can't go on calling you Commander," she said. "It sounds stupid." She flashed Randal a look. "After all, you've never been my tutor. Haven't you got a name?"

Randal winced and waited for a blistering response. But the Commander only glanced at Damaris and said meekly, "Yes; it's Peregrin."

Damaris seemed unaware that she had been particularly outspoken.

"What I wanted to ask, Peregrin, is what do you think Veryan should do. He seems to listen to you, if he doesn't listen to anyone else. I'd like to help, but I don't want him getting himself arrested."

Frowning, the Commander finished easing a tiny strip of metal into place.

"What I think he should do first," he said at last, "is promise not to do anything without consulting the rest of us. We'll help you, Veryan—at least, I will, and I suppose? . . ." Randal and Damaris nodded. "Then you can rely on all of us. But we would prefer not to have to save you from the Warden's thugs. Is that agreed?"

Veryan gave him a wide-eyed, serious look. "Yes, Peregrin."

"Good. Then I'll make you your decoder while we all try to think of some way to get past the guards."

That evening all of the remaining staff of the center assembled for a meeting in the lounge. By the time Randal and the others arrived, the room was already crowded. But they managed to find seats at the back.

Veryan was still carefully shepherding the Commander who was exhausted after working all afternoon on the damaged machinery. Randal supposed he would have to get used to thinking of him as Peregrin. It did not feel as difficult as he would have expected. Somehow he was looking younger and more relaxed, as if in shedding the fleet rank he had shed a lot of other burdens along with it.

They were hardly settled when an older man whom Randal had not seen before got up to speak.

"I don't want to talk about what happened this morning," he began. "We all know far too much. But I would like to bring you up to date with what has happened since."

"Get on with it then," Damaris muttered.

"The best news is that we still have the water supply. If that goes off we can really start to worry. Our food supply is the next thing we have to sort out. No one in Altir will accept a credit code in payment and even money isn't as popular as it used to be." A few people laughed, though Randal could not see the joke.

"We're back to barter," the man went on. "So if any of you have ideas about what we could use, see me afterwards. We're going to ask for payment in food or other essentials for medical treatment, but only from patients who can afford it," he added, forestalling a murmur of protest. "And I don't suppose there will be many of those. Just one thing: drugs are not to be used for barter under any circumstances. We give them freely to those who need them, or not at all."

"I thought the store was smashed up," someone in the audience said.

"Yes, but we're salvaging what we can. You're right, though. That's going to be one of our biggest problems. We're out of some essentials and others will run out soon. And I don't see any possibility of getting more."

He paused, and then went on, "Another bit of good news is that we've found an expert who can repair our equipment." He waved a hand toward Peregrin who deliberately did not catch anyone's eye. "In fact, I've heard that some items are already back in working order." There was a ripple of applause. "I don't know how long the Warden will let us keep them going, but what he doesn't know won't hurt him. So don't talk about it outside the center."

For Randal, his words conjured up another mob attack like the first one. He tried not to think about it while the speaker went on at length about duty rosters and the jobs that were still to be done. Not being trained for anything else, Randal expected to be back with his mop the next morning.

Eventually, after a period for questions, the meeting broke up. Randal led the way back to the entrance hall.

"Damaris," Veryan was saying, "is there anywhere Peregrin can sleep? He really has to rest now."

"Let him have my bed," Randal said. "I can find—"

He broke off. In the middle of the entrance hall a shimmering curtain had flickered into being. It was about the size of a doorway, a quivering gray shot through with silver.

"A ship's teleport!" Randal exclaimed. "But who? . . ."

Two figures, a man and a woman dressed in gray fleet uniforms, stepped through the curtain. Both of them carried large containers made of metal. The woman set hers down, saluted, and addressed herself to the older man who had spoken at the meeting.

"Are you in charge here?" she asked. "We're from the *Pioneer*. We have a consignment of drugs for you."

Ignoring Damaris's joyful exclamation, Randal stepped forward and spoke to the man who still stood in front of the teleport.

"Lieutenant Reede?"

The man turned to him. "Oh, hello, Randal," he said. "Your father told us to look out for you."

After a lot of confusion and questions that went on for much longer than he thought was necessary, Randal found himself on board his father's ship. Damaris, Veryan, and Peregrin were with him. Lieutenant Reede escorted them to the Captain's quarters.

Randal felt his heart pounding uncomfortably. It was several months since he had seen his father. When he was shown into his sitting-room and his father got up to greet him, his first instinct was to fling himself forward and hug him. But that, he thought, would be childish. So he contented himself with standing very straight and saying, "Reporting for duty, sir."

The effect was rather spoiled by the wide grin that he could not keep off his face. His father nodded, smiling.

"Welcome aboard. And this, I suppose, is Veryan? And your other friends?"

Damaris stepped forward, her hand extended to shake.

"Damaris Arden, sir. Randal and I have been working together at the medical center."

Captain Gray greeted her and then turned enquiringly to Peregrin.

"Peregrin Farre, sir," Peregrin said. His tone was stiff, and he offered no more explanation of who he was. The Captain gave him a sharp glance.

"Don't I know you?"

"No, sir."

Randal realized this could be the first time Peregrin had been on board a ship since he was rescued after the loss of the *Valiant*. He could understand why he might feel ill at ease.

"Commander Farre?" the Captain asked. "First officer of the *Valiant?*"

Peregrin admitted it with a curt nod.

"I'm proud to meet you," the Captain said. He held out a hand. Reluctantly, Peregrin shook it. "They decorated him, you know," the Captain went on. "The Silver Cross. He stayed at his post with the ship breaking up around him, getting off a distress call. Without that, none of the survivors would have been picked up." Veryan gave Peregrin a glowing look, and moved closer to his side.

"I didn't want it," Peregrin said. "There were others who deserved it more."

"Well, we won't go into that," the Captain said, seeming to realize for the first time that there was something wrong with Peregrin. "And then they grounded you? We won't go into that, either. Come and sit down, all of you."

He indicated a group of chairs around a low table on the other side of the room. Randal moved across with him, beginning to spill out all the story of everything that had happened. Most of it he confused and placed in the wrong order.

"Yes, yes," his father said, laughing, "we've got plenty of time to hear all that."

Damaris said, "I'd like some explanations first, sir. What are you doing here? And how did you manage to find Randal?"

"That's a long story too," Captain Gray said.

He waited until they had found seats. Randal caught him giving Peregrin another close scrutiny, as if wondering why he should look so tired and ill, but he made no comment.

"I suppose I'd better start at the beginning," he said.

At least Randal and Damaris were listening to him. Peregrin had sunk into the chair as if he were losing the struggle to stay awake, and Veryan had no attention to spare for anyone but him.

"You know why we're at war," Randal's father began. "Some of Earth's colonies are fighting for their independence, while others, like the Six Worlds, are fighting on the side of Earth. That's been going on so long that they're teaching it in the schools." He gave a sidelong glance to Randal, who was shifting impatiently in his seat. "Well, until recently it's all been happening a long way away. The fleet was involved, but the war didn't make much difference to the ordinary people of the Six Worlds. Now that's all changed."

"Why?" Damaris asked.

"Because the rebel fleet has been driving Earth back into its own system."

"You mean Earth is losing?" Randal asked indignantly. In all his thinking about the war, even after he had begun to worry about his father's safety, he had never considered the possibility that Earth—and therefore the Six Worlds—might lose. "That's impossible!"

His father gave him a tight smile. "Not impossible at all," he said. "But that's not the point. What matters is that this movement back toward Earth has meant that over the last few weeks a major battle has been fought in the Six Worlds system.

"Commander Farre could explain the strategy to you." He glanced at Peregrin, who was clearly not in a fit state to explain anything to anybody. "The enemy don't attack other ships, not if they can help it. They attack strategic points on the ships' home world so that the back-up systems are destroyed and the ships are isolated and helpless. That's what's been happening here."

"On the other worlds, too?" Damaris asked.

"Yes. And along with the attacks from space, we know there are enemy agents on the ground. With a population close to panic, they can stir up trouble and maybe even persuade people to destroy their own installations. . . ."

"I see!" Damaris interrupted. "Then the Warden is one of the enemy? We should tell—"

"No," the Captain interrupted in turn. "The enemy doesn't work like that. The man in charge will certainly be someone from Barren, but look among his close advisers. . . ."

"Then that's what we should do!" Damaris was on her feet, eager for action. "If we can prove to people that the enemy are making them smash everything—"

"But how do you prove it?" the Captain asked. "Sit down, Damaris. They're not aliens, you know. We were all one people once. And if there is an agent, he'll have a good cover story."

Damaris sat down again. Her face showed that she had to accept what the Captain told her. But she was very far from liking it.

"Now," the Captain said, "the battle is over, I think for good. I don't expect any more attacks from space. Though the trouble on the ground will go on for some time yet, I'm afraid. The most important thing that has only just happened is that the Six Worlds have lost all contact with Earth."

"How is that possible?" Randal asked.

"All their ships have withdrawn toward their own system. They don't answer radio calls. Personally, I think they have all the trouble they can handle without worrying about the Six Worlds."

"You mean Earth has just . . . abandoned us?" Randal asked disbelievingly.

"Yes. They may have had no choice. But there's been a meeting of the War Council on Centre and they have decided that until the situation changes we will expect no further help or support from Earth."

"So we got our independence after all," Peregrin said drowsily.

Randal was surprised. He had not thought Peregrin was listening.

"Yes," his father said. "Though it remains to be seen what we can do with it. At present, we have to concentrate on salvaging what we can from the attacks. The fleet has been recalled to Centre, and we're coordinating everything from there.

"So now I can answer the question you asked at first. I spoke to your mother on Centre—and yours, Veryan. And of course we were all very worried about you, so when this assignment came up for a ship to distribute drugs and other medical supplies to the trouble spots on Barren, I volunteered for it. Pulled strings, called in a few favors, that sort of thing. I was hoping I would be able to locate you, though I didn't expect it to be quite so easy."

"Then my mother's still on Centre?" Veryan asked, his relief showing in his face.

CHAPTER 20

"Yes. There were no civilian flights to bring her home. She's perfectly all right and she'll be even better when she knows that you're safe."

"But, sir, I haven't told you—"

As quickly as he could, Veryan explained to the Captain how the Governor was a prisoner in his own residence and under sentence of death. Captain Gray listened thoughtfully.

"I hadn't expected this," he admitted. "I thought I would just get you off safely to Centre."

Veryan assumed the obstinate expression that by now was familiar to Randal, though he spoke with all his accustomed politeness.

"I can't do that, sir," he said. "I feel . . . responsible. I must try to do something to help. Randal? . . ."

"Yes, of course I'll come," Randal said. "I think you're out of your mind, but I'll come. If you'll let me," he added to his father, remembering that it might be well to ask permission first.

His father gave him a slow, reluctant smile. "You've been making your own decisions for a while now," he said. "You may as well go on doing it. If your mother were here, she would say the same."

"Can you help us?" Randal asked eagerly.

"I can't send the troops in," his father said, still with a faint smile. "I've got my assignment to complete and I'm behind schedule already. You're really prepared to go down there?" he asked Veryan.

"Yes, of course," Veryan answered promptly.

"You can't teleport through a defense screen," Randal objected.

"I've got the decoder Peregrin made," Veryan said.

"Which won't work at this range," the Captain pointed out. "What I can do is teleport you into the garden, inside the circle of guards. Then you deactivate the screen, get the Governor out, and I'll pick you up again."

Damaris was on her feet again, impatient to be moving.

"Good," she said. "I'm coming, too."

"So am I," said Peregrin. The Captain stared at him.

"You're not fit," he said. "The only place you should be is in sick bay. I've a good mind to order you there right now."

Peregrin pulled himself to his feet. "I'm not under your orders. Sir," he added after a pause. He and the Captain measured glances, until Peregrin turned aside to Veryan. "Veryan saved my life," he said. "He's not going down there without me."

Captain Gray hesitated for a little longer and then let out a long sigh.

"Have it your own difficult way," he said. "I wish I had you under my command, that's all. Now listen." He spoke to all of them. "This is a dangerous operation. I'll put you down, but I daren't hold the teleport. I can't risk the Warden's men on board this ship. I'll give you a radio, and you can tell me when you're ready to be picked up. With the screens down, I can teleport you out of the house. If I don't hear from you, I'll open the teleport in the same place exactly one hour from when I put you down. If you miss that rendezvous . . ." Again he hesitated and then continued, "I'll do my best to find you. But I can't stay in orbit around Barren for ever. Just don't miss the rendezvous, all right?"

21

It was late that night when they stepped through the teleport into the garden of the Governor's residence. As the entrance faded behind him, Randal stood cautiously looking around.

The city was dark except for faint and flickering lights here and there. Even people who still had their own power packs would not dare to use them for light at night. In the distance was the dark smolder of a burning building.

Randal could make out lights at the gatehouses that flanked the main entrance. The guards were out of sight, but he knew they would be there. Other guards were posted at intervals around the walls. But the garden was large. There would be no need to go near them and no reason they should be alerted.

He glanced at the watch his father had given him, set to ship's time. Two minutes of their promised hour had passed. Already Veryan had begun to move toward the house.

"Stay off the path," Damaris advised in a low tone. "Use the bushes for cover."

They did as she suggested, Veryan leading with Damaris, followed by Peregrin, and Randal bringing up the rear, making sure that he had marked the spot in his mind in case they had to return to it. He tried to listen, especially for danger coming up from behind, but he could hear nothing except their own quiet footsteps and the sigh of the wind in the trees.

They were approaching the house when Randal saw Damaris stop abruptly. She grabbed Veryan and dragged him into the cover of the shrubbery. She beckoned urgently for Randal and Peregrin to join them. Crouching, peering through the leaves,

Randal could see the open space that surrounded the house.

On the landing pad was a twisted wreck that had once been a flyer; Randal could just make out the official flashes on the crumpled wings, and guessed it was the one the Governor had used on his visit to the mountain house. But the flyer took no more than a second of Randal's attention. Standing beside it was one of the Warden's guards.

The man began to advance cautiously, his eyes fixed on the clump of bushes where they were hiding. Randal realized, with a twist of fear inside him, that he must have seen or heard something that had aroused his suspicions.

"Who's there?" he called. From his belt he drew a long knife. "Who's there?" he repeated. "Show yourself!"

They crouched, frozen. If they tried to retreat they would give away their position. If they stayed where they were, they would be discovered, their attempt to rescue the Governor a failure before it had really begun.

There was another shout from the guard. Randal heard an answering shout, and two other guards hurried up from different directions.

We should have known, he thought, *they wouldn't just have guards on the wall*.

The three guards together began to advance purposefully toward the bushes. Randal braced himself to fight his way out. But before he could launch himself into an attack that he knew would be hopeless, Peregrin suddenly straightened up and stepped into the open.

"Very well," Randal heard him say in the cool, disdainful voice he knew so well. "I don't choose to be dragged out. What can I do for you, gentlemen?"

The guards closed around him. Veryan took a breath to cry out, and Damaris clamped a hand hard over his mouth.

"No!" Her voice was a furious undertone. "He did it to help us. You'll ruin it if you give yourself away."

Veryan's face changed enough for Damaris to release him. Beyond their shelter the guards were roughly questioning Peregrin and searching him. One of them pulled something out from the inner pocket of his jacket. Damaris closed her eyes in anguish.

"The radio!" she breathed.

"What's this?" the guard was asking. Peregrin's voice was icy.

"You can see what it is."

"And where did you get it?"

Silence.

One of the other guards suggested, "Stole it, like as not. Let's take him down to the sergeant, and question him properly."

They began to drag Peregrin away down the path to the main gate. Veryan scrambled to his feet and Randal put out a hand, warning him, afraid he would try to follow. Veryan was distraught, trembling.

"We can't let them take him!" he said.

Randal wanted to say something reassuring, but he was at a loss.

It was Damaris who said, "I'll follow them and see what they do. You two get into the house and find the Governor. Leave the screen down so that I can get to you if I have to. If we can't get the radio back we'll have to make the rendezvous."

She was gone, silently slipping down the path after Peregrin and the guards. Reluctantly recognizing the good sense in what she said, Randal pulled at Veryan's arm.

"She's right. Come on."

Veryan, struggling for self-control, allowed himself to be drawn across the open space toward the house. Randal was alert for more guards, but there was no movement and he guessed that the three who had gone with Peregrin were the only ones on duty. Meanwhile Veryan had taken out Peregrin's decoder, and was keying in the sequence of numbers that would deactivate the defense screen. Randal had no time to wonder whether the decoder would work, before the faint shimmer in the air, the only visible sign of the screen, faded. Swiftly, Veryan crossed the open space, keyed in another sequence of numbers on the door panel, and entered the house.

Randal slipped into the entrance hall behind him. Everything was dark. Veryan put out a hand to activate the lights, and then snatched it back.

"The guards would see us," he murmured. "We should have brought a torch."

A narrow beam of white light cut the darkness as Randal snapped on a tiny penlight.

"I asked my father for it," he explained.

Veryan closed the door and Randal led the way farther into the house, careful not to let the light show in any of the windows. Already he was feeling uneasy. The darkness and silence were unexpected. Besides, even if he had not heard the disturbance outside, the Governor should have realized by now that the screen had gone down and someone had entered the house. Why had he not come to investigate?

The residence was large. They moved through it like shadows, shielding the penlight beam. Their movements were as silent as they could make them. They scarcely dared speak. Their search took them through the Governor's office and the rooms for official functions, through the rooms where the family lived, through the paved courtyard where the fountain no longer played, through the kitchen and bathrooms and storerooms. Soon they began to realize the truth. And when the search came to an end in the Governor's private study, they had to accept it. Apart from themselves, the house was empty.

"This doesn't make sense!" Randal said, his frustration seething through his whispered tones. "Where has he gone?"

"Perhaps he was never here," Veryan suggested. "But everyone said . . ."

"Then the rumors must be wrong," Randal replied. "No one ever saw him, after all."

"Then where is he?" Veryan was growing distressed again and his voice was shaking. "What are we going to do?"

"Not panic, to begin with." Randal put an arm round Veryan's shoulders. "Listen. If he was here, he might have left a message for you. Where would he have put it?"

Veryan thought. "I'm not sure. He would always send messages through the servants. But I suppose he might have . . ."

His voice died away. He took the penlight from Randal and began to hunt around the desk and the bookshelves. Randal watched him. Everything in the room was meticulously tidy and clean except for a fine film of dust on the polished surfaces. There was nowhere obvious where a message could have been left.

"I'll tell you something else," Randal said as Veryan continued to search. "A lot of the house equipment has gone, particularly the electronics."

"Then maybe the Warden's men have been here already," Veryan said.

"How did they get past the screen? Besides, they would have smashed everything and burned all of this." He waved a hand at the towering shelves. "The built-in equipment, like the door controls, is still working. But everything moveable has gone. Who took it?"

Randal was still thinking that over and failing to come up with an explanation when Veryan gave up his search.

"There's nothing," he said. "Randal, what do we do now?"

Randal took him by the shoulders. This time he was not going to listen to any arguments.

"We find Damaris," he said. "And then we try to get Peregrin out, make our rendezvous and leave." As Veryan tried to protest, he went on forcefully, "You've done all you can, and more than anyone could expect. The Governor isn't here. He could be anywhere on the planet—or off it, for that matter. He isn't your responsibility anymore."

"Oh, I suppose you're right," Veryan admitted. "But I can't—"

He broke off with a gasp, and swung around. The light angled wildly toward the door as a soft footstep sounded behind him.

"It's all right. It's only me," Damaris said. She was tense with an excitement that alerted Randal. "I've been down at the gatehouse," she added. "And the guards are keeping a better watch than we thought. They've noticed that the defense screen is down. They're moving in."

22

Randal's first thought was to reactivate the screen, but he quickly realized how useless that would be. They would be safe from the guards, but they would be trapped in the house. Then they would be unable to reach the rendezvous point in the garden and unable to do anything to help Peregrin. He glanced at his watch. Less than fifteen minutes of their hour remained.

"Where is Peregrin?" Veryan was asking. "Have they hurt him?"

"No," Damaris reassured him. "But I think they've smashed the radio. The good thing is they're bringing him up here with them. They know something is going on and that he's involved with it."

Randal thought again. To reach the rendezvous point they would have to pass the guards. It might be possible to slip out unobserved, but that would mean leaving Peregrin behind.

Slowly he said, "We'd better be prepared to be stopped and questioned. Are we carrying anything that will get us arrested?"

Damaris patted herself and shook her head. Randal unfastened his watch and checked the time again before slipping it into a desk drawer. Not much more than ten minutes. Veryan switched off the torch and put it in the same drawer.

"What about the decoder?" Randal asked.

"I was forgetting."

Veryan opened his jacket and took the decoder out of an inside pocket. Even in the near darkness Randal could see that it was not the only thing he had forgotten.

"What about this?" He reached into Veryan's pocket and took out his father's Bible.

Veryan stared at it. "But that's—"

"That's a violation of the Fifth Edict," Damaris informed him. "How long have you been carrying it around?"

"I always carry it."

"Give me strength!" Damaris exclaimed. "Did you have it this morning in the riot?" Veryan nodded, bewildered. "You realize that if anyone had seen it, you could have been torn to pieces?"

Veryan obviously did not realize anything of the sort. Damaris finally gave up trying to convince him.

"Put it on a shelf," she said to Randal, "and let's get out of here."

Randal was turning to the bookshelves when Veryan darted up behind him and snatched the book out of his hand.

"But they'll burn it." A betraying quiver in his voice, he added, "It was my father's. It's all I have."

Randal put a hand on his arm comfortingly. "You don't need it now," he said.

"Are you going to stand here all night?" Damaris asked impatiently.

She slipped out of the room. Veryan was still clasping the book to him, desperately uncertain of what he ought to do. Randal glanced around the study. Once the Warden's guards got in they would smash and burn. Was there any way of hiding the book so that it would survive?

"I know!" Randal exclaimed. He brought out from the desk a metal box that held a few papers. He tipped the papers out.

"Put it in here," he said. Veryan met his eyes doubtfully. "We'll hide it and you can come back for it later," Randal explained.

Suddenly making his mind up, Veryan obeyed, laying the book in the box. Randal locked it and handed Veryan the key.

"You keep that," he said. "They'll never think twice about a key."

Now they had to find a good place to hide the box. An idea came to Randal. With Veryan following him, he groped his way into the passage and from there to the courtyard. On the way Damaris joined them again.

129

"The house is surrounded," she reported. "But they're keeping their distance. Maybe they think we have weapons."

"I wish we did," Randal muttered.

In the courtyard, he knelt at the edge of one of the paving stones and pulled up the clump of flowers that grew beside it.

"Gardening?" Damaris asked.

Ignoring her, Randal jammed the box into the hole he had made, managing to force it under the overhang of the stone. Then he pushed the plant back on top of it.

"There!" he said. "Even if they burn the house down, it should be safe."

Veryan was looking relieved. "I'm sorry," he said. "I know I'm being stupid, but . . ."

"No, it's all right." Surprisingly, it was Damaris who spoke without her earlier irritation. "But you haven't lost anything, you know. You can't shut God up in a box."

Randal got to his feet again. He was missing the watch, but he knew there could only be a few minutes to go before the rendezvous. He took a deep breath.

"Come on," he said. "Let's go."

They slid silently down the arched passageway that led to the back of the house. In the shadows they paused. The Warden's guards were strung out along the edge of the open space, their backs to the garden, watching the house. Randal could see that they wanted to attack, but they were afraid to come closer. There was no sign of Peregrin.

"This is no good," Damaris whispered. "We've no time to stand skulking here."

To Randal's dismay, she stepped out of the shelter of the passageway and walked firmly toward the guards. Randal bit back a protest and gripped Veryan's arm.

"This is it," he murmured. Together they moved into the open and followed Damaris.

By the time they caught up with her, she was replying to a question barked out by the nearest guard.

"We were looking for the Governor," she said. Then, as Randal wondered why she had chosen this particular moment to tell the truth, she added, "He failed the people of Altir. He deserves to be punished."

And that was the truth, too, Randal reflected. Except that by phrasing it like that, Damaris had suggested she was a faithful follower of the Warden, somebody that the guards might praise for her enthusiasm.

"You're out after curfew," the guard said uncertainly.

"I know." Damaris studied her feet, and shot the guard a look of charming embarrassment. "Maybe we did wrong. But we wanted to help so much."

Randal allowed himself an inward grin. He would not let Damaris forget this performance in a hurry! Meanwhile, a second guard rapidly searched all three of them and found nothing to complain about.

"Have you been in the house?" he asked.

"Yes, but we didn't find anything," Damaris replied.

"Except a lot of books," Randal said, and added virtuously, "You will burn those, won't you?"

The second guard had moved away down the line, shouting orders. The guards began to move forward.

"You stay here," the first guard said, "if you want to see burning. We'll talk about the curfew later," he promised.

"Not if we can help it," Damaris murmured.

The guards reached the house and began to enter. Now that no weapons were unleashed against them, Randal, Damaris, and Veryan found themselves alone again with no one paying much attention to them. As unobtrusively as they could, they began to move to the front of the house. Randal had the sensation of time rapidly running out, and they had still not found Peregrin.

Then they saw him. He was standing with his back against a tree. His face was blanched in the moonlight, the scar very prominent. He looked as if the tree might be all that was keeping him upright. Two men were standing guard over him.

Quietly Damaris worked her way behind trees and bushes until she stood only a few feet away from Peregrin. Randal and Veryan followed. The guards had their backs to her as she ventured out from cover again. Randal caught a sudden alertness in Peregrin's face as he saw her. At the same moment, a gray shimmer in the bushes over to his left told him that the teleport had appeared.

Randal placed his lips close to Veryan's ear.

"Go," he whispered. "Tell them to hold on."

Veryan gave one anguished look at Peregrin and obeyed. Relieved that he at least was out of danger, Randal kept close to Damaris's side as she crept nearer to the guards. He was ready to spring, but at the last instant his foot slipped on a root. One of the guards spun around. He was holding a knife. Randal dived toward him under the blade, grabbed at him, and brought him crashing down into the undergrowth.

The man was yelling something and struggling to free himself. Randal could not do much more than hold on, trying not to think of where the knife might be. He felt a hand fasten in his hair and his head was wrenched back. His grip on the guard relaxed. The man slithered away from him and before Randal could do any more, he had found his feet and was running across the open space toward the house.

Randal turned. Behind him, Peregrin and Damaris had managed to dispose of the other guard who lay motionless on the ground.

"Have we killed him?" Damaris asked.

"No," Peregrin replied. "But he'll wake up with a headache. I can't say I'm sorry."

He staggered suddenly, his injured leg refusing to support him. Randal went to his side. "Come on," he said. "Quickly, while the teleport is here."

He could still see the gray shimmer among the trees. They made for it, but the brief struggle with the guard had taken the last of Peregrin's strength and he was very slow. Glancing over his shoulder, Randal could see more guards come swarming out of the house. The teleport entrance was growing closer, but Randal did not know if they could reach it before the guards caught up with them. Peregrin's face was set with the effort he was making.

Then Veryan appeared from the teleport, and behind him

two of the ship's troopers with stun pistols in their hands. They aimed their weapons high over the heads of the guards and their rush was halted. In the few seconds' respite, Randal plunged for the entrance. He felt the tingling shock as he passed through it and felt the smooth metal of the ship under his feet instead of the earth of the garden. They were through. Veryan and the troopers followed and the entrance faded, leaving only the blank wall of the ship. In the last instant, Randal had caught a glimpse of flame leaping beyond the trees as fire devoured the house.

hat do you mean, I can't go back?" Damaris asked. In the *Pioneer's* teleport room she confronted Captain Gray, her expression dangerous.

"I mean that we've already left orbit," the Captain explained. "Next stop, Centre."

"But I have work to do! I can't just abandon all the people at the medical center."

"I'm sorry," the Captain said. "I thought I'd made it clear. I've already bent my orders so far that they're unrecognizable. Besides," he added, "no one is abandoning Barren or any of the other Worlds. It's just a question of whether you want to continue struggling along by yourself, or be part of a properly organized relief program. Is your family in Altir?"

"No," Damaris said. "But they are on Barren. They're not exactly expecting me to go off planet."

The Captain smiled. "All the same, they might be delighted to hear that's where you are. Go and see if you can get through to them on the radio."

"May I? Now?" Damaris asked, her expression changing. "I haven't talked to them for days. They must be worried sick."

Captain Gray gestured to one of the crew members standing by. "You should be able to get through from here," he said.

Pacified, Damaris followed the crew member out. Captain Gray turned his attention to Peregrin.

"Under my orders or not," he said, "you're going to sick bay."

"There's absolutely nothing wrong with me," the Commander said. He was supporting himself against the wall, his face gray, his protest unconvincing.

"I'm delighted to hear it," the Captain said. "When my Chief Medical Officer is as certain as you are, she'll let you out. Until then, behave yourself."

Peregrin drew himself up, looked as if he were going to protest again, and then shrugged resignedly. "Very well, sir."

Randal passed the next few hours in a blur. Later he remembered eating, taking a shower, and crawling into bed. But it was not until the following day that he started to think about the future.

With Damaris and his father, he visited the Commander in sick bay. Veryan was already there. He had managed to find a small chess set and they were both absorbed in the game. Peregrin still looked worn, but he was recovering some of his old spirit. Veryan put the chess set aside as the others came in.

"Everything all right?" the Captain asked.

"Oh, yes, sir, thank you," Veryan replied enthusiastically. "It's wonderful to be here. I never expected I would be able to go off planet." He gave the Commander his mischievous smile. "Peregrin said space is boring."

"I thought his problem was that he found it too exciting," the Captain remarked.

"It is boring in here," Peregrin said, with an acid look at the Captain. "Sir, will you take Veryan up to the observation deck and show him something of how the ship works? He shouldn't spend the whole voyage keeping me company in this sick bay."

With a confidence that astonished Randal, Veryan reached out and took Peregrin's hand affectionately.

"Don't be absurd," he said.

"There's plenty of time," Captain Gray said. "In a few days, Commander, you'll be out of here, and then you can show him yourself."

A spot of color appeared in the Commander's face as he tried to hide how pleased he was.

"You can show all of us," Damaris said, sitting down on the end of his bed. "I never expected to be in space either. At least, not as soon as this. And certainly not kidnapped!"

She was laughing up at the Captain. He smiled back at her.

"You spoke to your parents?" he asked. "Is everything all right?"

"Oh, yes. My father fussed a bit. But then, he always does. He'll get over it. I'll find my way home somehow, sooner or later. Or perhaps I can arrange to study on Centre."

"You may find that you won't be able to study anywhere else," Captain Gray told her. "What you've seen on Barren is happening all over the Six Worlds. I'd guess that there are some black years ahead of us. We're going to need people like you to help us recover and preserve what we can of the old life—yes, even you, Commander," he added, catching Peregrin's slight shake of the head. "We've lost too many good men from the fleet."

"I was discharged as unfit, sir," Peregrin said.

"Things have changed. A commission can always be reactivated."

Peregrin's eyes were wary. "I don't want that, sir. I don't want to fight again."

Exasperated, the Commander drew a breath. "Haven't you been listening to what I've been telling you? The war is over—for the Six Worlds, at least. It's passed us by. We've lost contact with Earth. It isn't fighting we want now, it's people to help us rebuild." He smiled down at the Commander so that Randal could see the warmth of his admiration for the younger man. "Be as difficult as you like," he said, "but when we get to Centre, I'm going to bring your case before High Command."

Peregrin ignored the remark. "And what about you?" he asked Randal, trying to divert attention from himself. "Still desperate to be a fleet cadet?"

"If they'll have me." For once, Randal was finding it hard to talk about his ambitions. He was not sure exactly when he had decided to take God seriously or why, except that all the people he had come to admire had got there before him. Awkwardly, he went on, "If not, I suppose God will find some use for me. I'll wait and see."

"Obedient at last!" the Commander said wryly.

"Being obedient doesn't count for much unless you have the

chance to be disobedient," Randal responded. "God doesn't force anyone, or He could have stopped the war and all the destruction from happening."

Damaris nodded reflectively. "Some of these people, even the Warden, might have thought they were doing the right thing. They might really believe that their way is best. Before we can obey, all of us have to learn what God wants us to do, and that isn't easy."

"You're not the first people to find that out," Captain Gray said.

Veryan had been listening seriously to all that the others had said.

"Do you think I might learn to be useful?" he asked diffidently. "I always thought I would never . . ."

"You're going to study," Peregrin interrupted sharply, "if I have to beat you three times a day."

Captain Gray was startled, more so when both Randal and Veryan dissolved into spasms of laughter. He looked at Damaris for an explanation, but she simply shrugged.

"They're both quite mad," she said.

"There's only one thing," Veryan said, sobering quickly. "One thing I have to do first. I must find out what has happened to the Governor."

Randal stepped out of the main entrance of Fleet Headquarters in Derinath on Centre. The sun was going down. He stood for a moment, enjoying the cool, fresh air, and the view of flowering trees in the park across the road. He felt tired and a little anxious, but mostly satisfied.

Soon he crossed the road and went into the park. On a bench nearby, two women were sitting, tossing crumbs to the birds. One of them was his mother. The other looked just like her, except she was slightly taller and her hair, instead of being black, was Veryan's dark copper.

Both women looked up as he approached.

"Well?" his mother asked. Randal flopped down on the bench and gave out a long sigh.

"Come on," his mother said. "You've been in there all day. What happened?"

Randal grinned.

"I filled in about three miles of forms," he said. "And I did a whole load of tests." He grimaced. "Computer studies. It's a good thing I had some more coaching from Peregrin on the way here. And I had four interviews. They all said, 'Randal Gray. Are you any relation to Captain Gray?' I think I'm in, but I'm not sure it's for the right reasons."

"Then you'll have to show them, won't you?" his mother said.

His Aunt Anya scattered the last of the crumbs and then they all got up and strolled along the path. Randal hurried on a few paces ahead. Veryan had been seeing the University authorities on the same day and they had arranged to meet in the park.

Soon he saw his cousin standing in front of a large piece of bronze sculpture, eyeing it with a doubtful expression.

"No, you're not drunk," Randal assured him. "It really looks like that." He linked his arm with Veryan's and said, echoing his mother, "Well?"

Veryan turned a glowing face to him.

"They accepted me! I have to do a preliminary year, 'to fill in the gaps in my education,' they said. I don't have to decide what to specialize in until I've done that."

He pulled away from Randal and turned to his mother as she approached, repeating his news to her.

"Wonderful!" his mother exclaimed. "Veryan, I can't believe I'm hearing this. I used to think that you would never . . . but it just shows how wrong I was." A little sadly, she added, "I'm sorry."

Veryan hugged her. "It wasn't your fault! It was me, and . . . well, a lot of other things. Let's not think about that now."

Randal could see he did not want to talk about his dead father. They walked on again, two and two. And this time Veryan laid a hand on Randal's arm and held him back as their mothers drew ahead.

Quietly, he said, "Randal, I've seen the Governor."

"What!"

Veryan gave a worried glance toward his mother.

"I don't want her to hear. I promised the Governor I wouldn't tell her. He wants to speak to her first."

"But what did he say to you?" Randal asked impatiently. "Where has he been? Where did you meet him?"

Veryan chose to answer the last question first. "At the University, when I went for my interview. Someone in the High Master's office had realized who I was and told him. He came to talk to me."

Randal could imagine that was the last thing Veryan would have wanted just before an important interview. But he did not suppose the Governor would have cared about that.

"So what has he been doing?" he asked. "Where was he when everyone thought he was in the residence?"

"On board a ship," Veryan replied. Randal stared. "When the attack came, there was a ship assigned to take all the important people off Barren—to form a kind of government in exile, I think. They came for the Governor. . . ."

"And he left you behind!" Randal exclaimed indignantly.

Veryan cast another glance at his mother, but by now the two women were well out of earshot.

"Not intentionally. What happened was that the ship's crew stripped the house of all the machinery. That's because so much is being destroyed, even here on Centre. And he left the house screened in case he could go back one day."

"If he does, he's going to get a nasty shock," Randal murmured.

"No, because I told him. Then he got them to put him down by teleport at the mountain house, but by then we had left. The housekeeper couldn't tell him where we were. And he couldn't do any more. The ship had other people to pick up and a schedule to keep. He did the best he could."

Randal grunted. He was not convinced. "You could be dead for all he cared."

"No, I think he was sorry. Shocked, too. And I don't think he's looking forward to meeting my mother."

"I can't say I blame him."

Randal was surprised that Veryan could take it all so calmly. He knew that his own parents would not have shrugged off their responsibilities so easily. Perhaps the difference was that the Governor was not Veryan's real father. Yet Veryan had risked his own life and his chance to escape from Altir when he thought the Governor was a prisoner in his own house. Blood relationship had nothing to do with it Randal decided. The Governor had failed Veryan just as he had failed the people of Altir because that was the sort of man he was.

"I'm glad it happened like that," Veryan was saying. "If we'd been picked up from the mountain house we wouldn't have found Damaris or Peregrin." He touched Randal's arm, and pointed. "Look."

Across the smooth grass was a fountain and on the stone rim Damaris was sitting, a hand held out into the spray. Another familiar figure stood beside her. Randal and Veryan veered across the grass toward them. Damaris caught sight of them and waved.

"I've been to the medical school!" she called. "I start next month!"

Next minute they had come up to her, and were spilling out their own news while Peregrin looked on good-humoredly. When Randal paused for breath, he saw that Peregrin was wearing a fleet uniform again. It seemed to have a lot of braid on it and the ribbon of his Silver Cross.

"You're the Commander again!" he said exultantly.

Peregrin looked embarrassed. "Actually, they seemed to think it was necessary to promote me," he confessed. "It's Captain now. But still a ground job," he added. "Coordinating communications between the Six Worlds. We're one people, not six, and we have to stay that way."

Peregrin was right, Randal knew. Just now, the excitement of being on Centre was enough for him. But he would never forget his home on Barren or his friends. He wondered what had happened to them and to everyone who had to face up to life after the attacks—Emrys and Mira at the farm, Dr. Sorel and Dr. Mayne, and all the staff at the medical center. He could do nothing for them except to find a useful place he could fill. But he knew now that God would not forget them.

The storm of war had swept over the Six Worlds, just like the storm when he and Veryan had climbed the mountain. They had faced danger, but out of it had grown their friendship. Perhaps something new would begin to grow for the Six Worlds.

"The Six Worlds," Veryan murmured, almost echoing Randal's thoughts. "Whole worlds, making their own decisions now. I wonder where we're going? I used to think I'd stay all my life in the house in Altir. And now . . ." He had an intent look. The others fell silent and listened. Realizing it, Veryan gave a little self-conscious laugh. "I don't expect I'll ever go back. I wonder if anyone will ever find the Bible? I wonder what it will mean to them if they do?" Laughing again more confidently now, he took Peregrin's arm. "I don't suppose we'll ever know."

Cradoc's Quest

"Life must be more than this."

Legend tells of a Book and a belief that the ancestors
from Earth once held. It's an almost-forgotten
belief—until now. For reasons unknown to him,
Cradoc—a young farmhand who longs for something
more from life—is chosen to bring that belief back to the
people of the Six Worlds.

Cradoc discovers a copy of the Book, thought to have
been destroyed during the Black Years. It contains truths
that could cause the greatest upheaval in the history of
the Six Worlds. Cradoc must get the Book to a printer so
its truths may be widely read, but there are many who
will try to stop him—and destroy the Book—along the
way.

The people of the Six Worlds long ago lost contact with
Earth and the belief of its people. Journey through the
Saga of the Six Worlds and discover, as they do, that
what's gone may not always be for good.

Cherith Baldry is involved with literature, especially
children's books, in all aspects of her life. She is a teacher
and school librarian and has two children of her own.
She and her family live in England where she enjoyes
writing, reading, and gardening.

Chariot Books
A Division of Cook Communications

Rite of Brotherhood

"You must do what you can to stop this war."

Aurion leaves his home on Two Islands as a hostage of the Tar-Askans, but he also goes to Tar-Askar as an ambassador.

The people of Tar-Askar have long-ago forsaken the ways of the peace-loving God of their ancestors, and now worship the god of power and war, Askar. Aurion is convinced that the way to prevent the war the Tar-Askans are preparing for is to turn them back to worshiping God. He plans to start with Arax, the king's son and his distant cousin. When he meets Arax, however, he wonders just how wise a choice he made.

The people of the Six Worlds long ago lost contact with Earth and the belief of its people. Journey through the Saga of the Six Worlds and discover, as they do, that what's gone may not always be for good.

Cherith Baldry is involved with literature, especially children's books, in all aspects of her life. She is a teacher and school librarian and has two children of her own. She and her family live in England where she enjoyes writing, reading, and gardening.

Chariot Books
A Division of Cook Communications